"This is certainly a peaceful place," observed Chan. "All the beasts living in harmony with each other. Maybe it really is a paradise."

They were just walking by a grove of spiky-leaved trees with trunks that looked like pineapples. Chan heard the crackling of something large displacing the foliage, and as he whirled around he saw a grotesque shape bearing down on him.

It was a huge lizardlike creature standing upright, though not erect, on heavily muscled rear legs. A long tail, held off the ground, balanced the weight of an enormous head. Its skin was green, darker on the back, set with small horny plates, the belly shading to ivory. Chan stood frozen, like someone in the path of an oncoming truck.

As he watched, the thing opened four-foot jaws. Its teeth were as long as knives . . .

DRAGON'S BLOOD

Alex McDonough

A Byron Preiss Visual Publications, Inc. Book

ACE BOOKS, NEW YORK

This book is an Ace original edition, and has never been
previously published.

DRAGON'S BLOOD

An Ace Book / published by arrangement with
Byron Preiss Visual Publications, Inc.

PRINTING HISTORY
Ace edition / October 1991

ISBN: 0-441-16627-X

Ace Books are published by The Berkley Publishing Group,
200 Madison Avenue, New York, New York 10016.
The name "Ace" and the "A" logo are trademarks belonging to
Charter Communications, Inc.

Chapter
1

*S*corpio felt triumphant as the skin of the orb-craft stretched into translucency. For the first time he felt as if he were gaining control of the strange time-traveling device. He looked over at Leah beside him as she stared at blurred shapes beyond the bubble-like wall formed by the orb. She had been brave, but he knew this jaunting from time to time was unnatural for her kind. Scorpio had promised her that he would return her to Avignon in her own time, the fourteenth century, and he wanted to see her face light with joy when she began to see familiar sights.

"Oh, Scorpio," she said, but with little of the delight he'd hoped for. As he turned his gaze to the surroundings outside the orb he saw why.

"This isn't Avignon," he said unnecessarily, as he studied the narrow street with its crowded open-air market and people dressed in unfamiliar costumes. There seemed to be a great many people in the street, and most of them were small with dark skins and hair, and almond-shaped eyes that gave them a mysterious look.

As the orb came to rest with feather lightness on the pavement, one of the vehicles they called a motorcar swerved around them at the last moment, blasting its horn. The car was alone on the street, among jostling foot traffic and many bizarre looking contrivances on two wheels. Some were powered with their own noisy engines like motorcars, but there were more of the kind that seemed to be run by human power. The word for bicycle appeared effortlessly from his subconscious. A working knowledge of the language was always provided by the orb. Scorpio couldn't imagine how riders kept these things upright in any case.

Just as he was marveling at these, another vehicle dashed by. It looked as if someone had mated a bicycle with a two-wheeled cart. The rider pedaled away furiously while a passenger rode in comfort behind.

Scorpio stared numbly at the scene, unaware that the orb bubble had burst, leaving himself and Leah on the busy street. He had worked so hard and was so sure that he was going to be successful this time—

He flinched when he felt Leah's hand on his arm.

"We'd better walk on, quickly," she said. "We're beginning to draw some attention."

Leah was only being polite by saying "we," Scorpio realized. Even in her heavy sheepskin coat she was not enough to make passersby stop and gape. Scorpio, with his tall, angular shape, rubbery gray skin and beaklike mouth had literally stopped traffic, he noted. People had gathered in groups to stare and point and jabber at each other, as vehicles and foot traffic halted, or worked their way between, causing even more confusion.

"This isn't a good situation," said Scorpio uncertainly. "Should we jump again?" He spoke halfheartedly, since when he contemplated another time jump, it was as if a thin black line, the edge of a pit of darkness, appeared at his feet. To use the orb would be to see that pit open before him.

That's strange, he thought. *I've never considered it in that way before.*

"Well—" said Leah hesitantly. Traveling together in the orb made them telepathic at times. He knew she realized he had no heart for trying again. Sharing feelings should have been comforting, but Scorpio only felt ashamed that his fear was on display. Since Scorpio was not able to control the orb after all, a new destination would not necessarily be an improvement over where they were now.

"There's really no need," said Leah. "The people seem curious, but not unfriendly. We should be able to escape their attention by simply walking away." Scorpio reached down to scoop up the orb, now only a small radiant sphere lying at his feet.

As they hurried along, Scorpio's strange appearance opening a way before them, they saw that this place was different from anything either of them had experienced. The city seemed well planned, but open-air market stalls were jammed between stores with glass windows as if old ways and new ways were in conflict. The airy architecture of buildings with a series of bright tile roofs leading up to a peak, the whole embellished with red and gold, existed side by side with ugly, no-nonsense structures of brick and stone. All these sights made Leah and Scorpio eager to know more. Scorpio felt a little better realizing that this was a pleasant place. With no imminent danger there was no need to think about jumping again so soon. His fears still nagged at him, but he pushed them to the back of his mind.

They walked down less-traveled streets until they had outpaced most of the curious. At last they found themselves in a small park. It was exquisitely landscaped, with unfamiliar trees laden with sweet blossoms of pink and scarlet, and well-kept beds of flowers. A clear stream was spanned by an arched bridge of wood with intricate carvings. They paused by an artificial pool rimmed with rock.

Scorpio leaned over to watch the lazily swimming fish, light filtering through the trees reflecting glints of gold from their scales. "At least we won't starve here," he said, reaching into the pool so swiftly the motion was almost a blur, and brought up a wriggling fish. Scorpio's people were aquatic, and it had been some time since he'd practiced his fishing skills. It pleased him that he hadn't lost his touch. He was about to pop it into his mouth, when he noticed Leah's squeamish look.

"Better put it back," she said. "We don't know what the rules are here and these fish are obviously here for ornamentation, not for eating. Even if I were hungry enough to join you, I'd want it cooked."

"Very well." Scorpio let the captive squirm free and fall back with a splash. "But let's at least take off these coats. They were just the thing for a Russian winter, but wherever this is, the climate is a much warmer one."

He gestured upward toward where the sun shone brightly in a cloudless blue sky.

They pulled off the hampering sheepskin coats, and Scorpio was about to toss his aside into a clump of bushes when Leah stopped him. "These are just about all we brought with us," said Leah. "That marketplace we just came from gives me an idea. I'll try to barter these coats. Maybe I can get something to eat or something to wear that'll make us look inconspicuous."

"Inconspicuous. That will be quite a feat," said Scorpio, "especially in my case."

"Less conspicuous, then," said Leah. "Don't leave this park, and if someone comes, find a place to hide. I'll be back as quickly as I can."

As Scorpio stood by the pool, he saw a man approaching.

His garment of saffron-yellow was wrapped about his body to leave one shoulder bare, and his head was shaven to the scalp except for a single long lock of hair on top. He carried a small white silk parasol against the glare of the sun. The parasol must have blocked his view, because he came straight toward Scorpio, not stopping until he had almost collided with him. The man looked surprised for a moment, and then regained his composure.

For a brief second Scorpio contemplated fleeing, but there was no place to run to, and the man looked gentle and harmless with his round, placid face touched with the hint of an enigmatic smile.

"I hope my appearance didn't startle you," said Scorpio.

"Appearance matters little," said the man. "We are always changing forms as we circle on the Wheel of Rebirth. You have existed before, in other ages."

"I don't know how you know that," said Scorpio, "but it's true. Before this, I was in the Russian Revolution. We were there when they stormed the Winter Palace."

"It's odd that you remember these things," said the man.

"Not so very odd," said Scorpio. "To me it was only yesterday. But I'm glad to be out of there. It was interesting, but dangerous."

A violent epoch," said the man. "No doubt you were killed there."

Scorpio began to edge away. "Sorry I can't stay and talk, but I just remembered an appointment."

"So you see that form is not important. It is *karma* that matters after all."

"Well, it's been enlightening." Scorpio hurried away. *He must have been walking around in the hot sun without his parasol,* Scorpio thought. *How does he think I could be talking to him now if I had been killed in Russia?*

When he looked back, he saw the man sitting by the pool

in what looked like a very uncomfortable position, knees bent and legs folded over each other.

Studying the lengthening shadows on the grass, Scorpio began to realize that Leah had been gone for some time. She had given him orders to stay hidden in the park, but he began to imagine her in trouble. After all, they knew nothing of the customs here. It would be easy to say something or do something to outrage the populace without even knowing it. Scorpio had traveled among humankind long enough to make that observation, and what he had observed on earth was usually on the violent side. He waited impatiently for several more minutes, and then decided to go out looking for Leah.

As he approached the marketplace, he saw that the street was now less crowded, and some of the merchants were packing up their goods evidently in preparation for going home for the night. With customers gone and the sellers busy about their tasks, Scorpio was able to advance along the street drawing only a few curious or alarmed stares.

Then, near a market stall where various fresh fruits and vegetables were displayed, he noticed a commotion that he hadn't caused. A fat man, whose girth was swathed in a long dirty apron, was dragging a struggling boy by one hand. The boy was very dirty and unkempt.

"I saw you steal those figs, you thieving monkey," the man was saying as he pulled the child along. "We'll see what the police have to say about this."

As Scorpio watched, three other children appeared. Shouting and shrieking, they converged on the fat man, and by grabbing hold of his clothing they tried to stop his progress down the street.

Like an ocean liner beleaguered by heavy waves, the man could continue by main strength, but his progress was now a slow one.

As the man finally lost his temper and began to slap at the children, Scorpio came forward, forgetting what effect his features might have on these people. "Be more gentle," said Scorpio. "Can't you see they're only young ones."

"Out of my way," growled the man, hearing Scorpio but not seeing him for the moment. His attention was on trying to drive away the children attacking him.

"You're going to hurt someone," cautioned Scorpio.

"I'm going to . . ." The man's voice wavered and fell silent as he turned and saw what was blocking his path. "What sort of creature is this?"

He cowered as Scorpio put out a gray-skinned, nailless hand to stop him. Looking wide-eyed at Scorpio for a moment, the captive boy recovered and took advantage of the situation to writhe free. The other children cheered him on, shrieking with excitement. They fled so quickly they might as well have been wraiths, but the merchant had now forgotten them and was shouting loudly, "Help, police! A monster! He's killing me!"

Scorpio looked at the man in amazement, since he hadn't even touched him. He was uncertain about what to do until he felt someone grasp his hand. He saw that it was Leah and she was holding a roll of cloth under one arm.

"What are you doing here picking fights with the natives? I told you to stay in the park out of sight."

"Picking fights? I was only trying to protect this little boy." He looked around, but none of the children were in sight.

The merchant's cries for help had finally had an effect as several people began to run toward them. Leah and Scorpio's thoughts meshed. *Run away! Hide!*

They pounded along the pavement, keeping a safe distance between themselves and their pursuers. Night was falling, and after a time they looked back and saw that the group behind them had dwindled. Finally no one at all was there. Evidently no one wanted to play hide and seek in dark alleys with two such outlandish creatures as Leah and Scorpio.

When they were certain that no one pursued, they stopped in the overhang of a building and Leah unrolled her parcel. Inside a woven mat she had two pairs of the gray pajama-like garments worn by many of the passersby—a sort of uniform of the poorer classes, Scorpio decided.

"What are these?"

"They called them Ho Chi Minh sandals," said Leah. The sandals were only soles crudely cut from automobile tires, tread-side down, with thongs to fasten them to the feet. "The peasant woman said they are easily come by, stick to the feet and last forever."

"Can't ask for more than that, I suppose," said Scorpio. "Didn't you get any food?"

Leah handed him a paper-wrapped bundle. Inside were balls of a sticky, brown-husked grain stuck together with fermented fish paste and some long fruit in a yellow skin. The word he wanted was "banana," Scorpio realized vaguely, too busy devouring the fruit to really care. Along with this was something in a hard, hairy husk. A hole had been bored in the top and a reed thrust in. Leah told Scorpio to suck on the reed. Inside was a sweet, thin liquid.

"Coconut milk," explained Leah. "And when you've drunk the milk, I can crack open the shell and there's a delicious white substance inside."

Scorpio had forgotten how hungry he was. The exotic food tasted like a banquet, even though they crouched in the dankness of a doorway.

Sated and now sleepy, Scorpio contemplated curling up on the pavement. "It should be warm enough here to simply sleep in the open," he said. "I'm strangely comfortable for having no idea where or when we are."

"That's what took me so long," said Leah. "I had quite a conversation with an old woman selling these rattan mats. "We're in a country called Cambodia. This is the capital city, Phnom Penh. It's built on a hill; that's what Penh means."

"But when are we?" asked Scorpio. "Did you find that out, too?"

"Yes. It's nineteen hundred and seventy-five. Imagine it! We've leaped all the years between."

Scorpio was getting sleepier.

"I don't have to imagine it," he said drowsily. "One day we're in Russia, the next in—what did you say they called this place?"

"Cambodia."

"At least they're not holding a revolution."

"They might as well be. The woman told me that war has been practically a way of life for these folk, since this is a small country with enemies on all sides. The Annamites or Vietnamese make regular raids across their borders, even though the country has declared its neutrality. And she said an evil empire from across the sea with its wicked king named Nix-On was attacking them from the air. I didn't understand that part. How could they be attacked by air, unless— No, that's too ridiculous."

"Why couldn't we have picked a place that's peaceful?" asked Scorpio choosing a corner to lie down in and pillowing his head on his arm.

"We didn't have that choice, remember?" said Leah, looking around fastidiously as if not thrilled by the prospect of sleeping in a doorway. Still, the night was velvet-dark and balmy. The scent of a flowering tree nearby drifted over them.

"It's strange, isn't it," he said, "how traveling through the nothingness between worlds makes one appreciate the sights, sounds and textures of a reality." Leah made a noncommital sound as she curled up in a corner of the doorway opposite him. He knew that with a little effort he could read her thoughts, but he didn't make the effort. Privacy was better, even between friends. Besides, if she was angry about being stuck here, he didn't want to know it.

Despite his exhaustion, Scorpio lay awake for a long time, trying to remember his own world, Terrapin. When the Hunters invaded his world, he had stolen one of their orbs, hoping that he could use it somehow to liberate his people. So far he had only bounced from one reality to another until now, or so it seemed, he had lost the courage to go on. He took the orb from its pouch and stared at its comforting glow. *It has healed others,* he thought. *Maybe it can give me the courage to jump back into the time stream, to try again.*

He clutched it tightly for several minutes, hoping to feel differently, but when he released it, he felt the same emptiness inside when he contemplated using the orb. *If I had a broken leg or a rash, things might be different,* he thought, *but some things are just too complicated. Some problems people have to solve for themselves.*

Scorpio and Leah were up before dawn the next morning. They used a row of shrubs as a dressing screen and put on the native garments. The remnants of their meal the night before served them as breakfast.

"We'll have to figure out some way to get food," said Leah. "We can't subsist on these crumbs, and we have nothing left to trade now that the coats are gone."

"While you were sleeping I was thinking," said Scorpio. "It's my fault that we're stranded here, and we can't live like this." He indicated the doorway. "But we're not quite without resources. We still have the orb."

"I hope you're not going to trade it for a few riceballs," said Leah.

"In a way," he said.

As they spoke, Leah became aware of a droning noise that was becoming ever louder. When she stepped from the shadow of the doorway, she saw it moving across the bright turquoise sky like something from a dream. Though she had been exposed to many wonders in her travels with Scorpio, her mind was still rooted in the fourteenth century, and the sight of the plane, glinting like silver as it moved rapidly through wisps of cloud, filled her with awe.

"The old woman I talked to wasn't crazy after all," she said. "People really can ride through the air."

Chapter 2

*T*hat afternoon Scorpio sat on the mat in the marketplace, his face covered by a length of gauze. He held the orb loosely before him. The small square of woven rattan was all the establishment the poorer merchants needed to sell their wares. *Now if it only works as I hope,* thought Scorpio.

"Scorpio, Seer of the Ages," Leah was saying loudly. "He will amaze and astonish you."

She stepped in front of a rapidly walking man. He had paler skin and more delicate features than those around him, and was dressed distinctively in a brown jacket and trousers. A long piece of cloth hung about his neck, though Scorpio could see no possible use for it.

"Excuse me, sir," Leah said. "Would you like a demonstration of Scorpio's powers?" A few passersby had already stopped and were gaping at the glowing orb.

"I haven't time," said the man, looking annoyed at first, and then looking at Scorpio with some amazement. "Some new dodge to fool the peasants?" he said. "All right, I suppose I can at least prove you're fakes before you get anyone's money.

Leah looked over her shoulder at Scorpio. Her expression was uncertain, as if to say that this would certainly make them look foolish if it didn't work.

"You must whisper your name to me," she said to the man. "Be very quiet so no one else hears."

Scorpio concentrated. The telepathic link between himself and Leah was there, established as they traveled together in the orb, but it wasn't necessarily dependable.

"Mr. Li Ng," said Scorpio aloud.

The small crowd that had gathered began to chatter among themselves, more from the high, warbling sound of Scorpio's alien voice than appreciation of his talents.

"That is correct," said Li Ng stiffly, "but I'm sure there is some explanation, such as a hidden radio receiver."

The crowd hooted in derision, but Leah faced them. "Wait, there's more. Mr. Li, please put some small personal object into my hand, but do not mention what it is."

There was a long silence as Leah and Scorpio concentrated. Some of the onlookers began to make rude noises.

"It's a . . . ring," said Scorpio. "In the shape of a serpent—no, a mythological creature. A dragon."

Leah opened her hand and showed the object to the crowd. Some of them cheered.

"Scorpio has the Wisdom of the Ages," said Leah for the crowd's benefit.

"For all we know this man is your stooge," said another onlooker, a soldier in a tattered uniform, a sidearm clipped to his belt. It was hard to forget Phnom Penh was near a war zone—the city was filled with soldiers.

"I've never seen them before in my life," said Li Ng.

"Come and tell me your name," said Leah.

When the demonstration was repeated and the soldier stood there dumbfounded, Leah said "Now, Scorpio, Seer of

Past and Future will answer your questions for a small gratuity."

Several in the crowd stepped forward eagerly.

Later, as they walked down the street toward a restaurant to spend some of their earnings, Leah said, "I'm not sure I like this way of getting money."

"Why not? Everything went perfectly, and we only took enough to meet our needs for the next few days."

"But I feel guilty. And what if people ask you questions about things important in their lives? You can't give them real answers."

"I'd never tell them anything that would do any real harm. If I give them a little hope, what can it hurt? Since it's my fault we're here, I'm going to make sure we live well."

"It also draws attention to us," said Leah. "By the time we were through, we'd gathered quite a crowd."

"Did you notice the group of children that arrived just before we were ready to quit for the day? I can't be sure, but they look like those who were struggling with the fat merchant."

"I was too busy to notice," said Leah.

"They were only there a short time, then they disappeared into the crowd."

Leah peered up at the buzzing and popping sign, letters outlined in garish pink light. It spelled out "EAT." Scorpio gaped at it a moment. "That's nothing," said Leah. I've seen so many wonders in my travels, I guess I'm becoming hard to impress. Besides, an establishment called 'Eat' doesn't inspire my confidence. I wonder if the food is good."

Two men were coming out of the place, so Leah went up to them and said, "I see you've just dined here. What's your opinion of the place?"

The man looked surprised, and with a smile at his companion, said, "This is the local hangout for foreign correspondents. You know journalists, they eat anything."

His friend laughed and they walked on. Leah peered puzzledly in through the door of the establishment, and saw that the place was full of people. She now understood the reference to foreigners, since most of those inside didn't resemble the natives.

"What are journalists?" asked Scorpio.

"It's another word for reporters. Do you remember when we covered the story of the capture of the Winter Palace by the Bolsheviks?"

Scorpio made the Aquay gesture of assent, a kind of sideways toss of the head that made it seem he were shaking off water drops. It had taken Leah quite awhile to recognize the gesture for what it was. "They don't seem to be doing much eating, despite the peremptory sign," he said.

Many of those inside were conferring together intently, their hands gesturing to make their points, as if they forgot they held fork or knife.

"Well, shall we go in?" asked Scorpio. "I'm getting hungry, and I think I'm at the point where I could eat anything, too."

"It's too crowded," said Leah. "There are surely some other places to choose from if we walk a little farther."

Despite Leah's worries, they continued the fortune-telling trade for the next few days, moving from location to location so people didn't get too curious about the glowing orb and the strange seer whose face was never seen. They prospered and were able to rent a cheap hotel room, then their luck ran out.

It was late afternoon and they were just about to bring the fortune-telling session to a close, when three soldiers appeared. They didn't appear ragged and exhausted as did

those who were usually seen loitering about the streets.
These were smartly arrayed in khaki uniforms with puttees.
At first they stood back and watched as Scorpio conferred
with a customer. Then, as if they had simultaneously made a
decision without speaking a word, they came forward.

"Would you like your questions answered by the Great
Seer?" asked Leah. The soldiers pushed by her and converged on Scorpio.

"We must ask you to come along with us, fortune-teller,"
said the tallest one, who seemed to be in charge."

"I wasn't doing anything wrong," said Scorpio. "Why are
you arresting me?"

"You're not being arrested," said the soldier. "In fact,
you're being honored. Our commander Lon Nol has heard
about your exploits, and he wants to confer with you."

"I suppose the three of you mean that I don't have any
choice in the matter."

"The choice to walk or be carried."

"Then I'll walk."

They started down the street, but Leah hastened to catch
up with them. "If you want the seer's powers to work at their
best, you must take me with you," she said.

"We'd better take her," said the leader. "This is one time
you won't want your powers to fail you. The commander
may be superstitious, but he's not stupid."

They were conducted to a place surrounded by a high
wall, the gate guarded by soldiers. Several regal-looking
structures stood amid well-kept lawns. Though they were
different in shape and size, all had broad flights of stairs
climbing to gilded doorways, painted walls with carven red
and gold shutters. Slim colonnades supported soaring eaves
and gables and many-tiered roofs rising to glittering spires.

They climbed a sweep of steps to a porticoed entrance and

were ushered inside by more guards. The hall they entered was almost bare of furnishings. What was there was exquisitely crafted, polished wood intricately carven and inlaid with lacquer and mother-of-pearl.

The soldiers who had brought them here stiffened to attention as a short, stout figure in a rumpled uniform appeared.

This Lon Nol in no wise belonged in these stately surroundings. Scorpio supposed the exigencies of war had ousted the officials who once used these rooms.

Lon Nol had the appearance of a rough-hewn clay idol. He had wrinkled dark skin and unruly black hair.

"So this is the mysterious seer," he said, approaching Scorpio. "Your reputation precedes you, so I hope I won't be disappointed. Why do you cover your face?"

"Uh, I was afraid my appearance might startle people."

"Do I look like I could be startled?" asked Lon Nol. "By anything?"

Scorpio unwound the gauze.

Several of the soldiers in the room couldn't suppress a sound of surprise, but Lon Nol's heavy-lidded eyes never even blinked.

"The rest of you can go," he growled at his staff.

"But your safety—" began a soldier, then quelled by a look, he too withdrew.

"Who is this?" he asked, indicating Leah.

"She's my trusted assistant," said Scorpio.

"Then I suppose she can stay." Lon Nol indicated seats on a low-slung couch. "The rumors mentioned a glowing sphere," he continued. "I would like to see it."

Reluctantly, Scorpio took the orb from its leather pouch and put it into Lon Nol's hands. The commander looked into its softly glowing depths contemplatively and said, "I hope you can help me."

This was a surprising comment from someone who was so accustomed to command. Scorpio and Leah were silent, and after a time he spoke again.

"You may know that an army is moving toward Phnom Penh. Not the Vietnamese or the Americans, this is an army of our own people. They organized in the jungles, in secret, but now their troops are everywhere. They threaten the capital itself.

"My men call them water crows because of their black pajama-style uniforms, but they call themselves only Angka, The Organization. The rumor is that they are a Communist organization: Khmer Rouge. Whatever the name, they fight like demons, and except for a miracle they'll overrun the city within the month." He looked up and gingerly passed back the orb as if its light burned him.

Scorpio and Leah exchanged looks. It was obvious to both of them that Lon Nol wouldn't be confiding internal security secrets to them if he intended to let them go after this.

"Angka works behind a screen of secrecy. Each small group knows some things, but few know all about the organization. Their true leaders remain anonymous."

"What do you want of me?" asked Scorpio. "I know nothing of wars."

"To kill a snake one must find the head. I know the officers and others ridicule my belief in the occult, but I'm akin to the old race, the pure Khmers who once ruled far beyond these borders. With a little belief, Cambodia might once again be great. I want you to use your powers to identify and locate the leaders of Angka. From what I've heard of you, and now seeing you, I believe you can do it."

Scorpio stammered a moment. He had been about to blurt out, "I don't know," but decided that wasn't a good answer for a seer. *Time, time,* he thought, then spoke aloud. "What you ask is not impossible, but I will have to rest, to gather all my powers so that I'll be up to the challenge."

"You will be given comfortable apartments, food and drink—whatever you want. In the morning I will consult with you again. I trust you'll be ready."

They were taken to a building nearby and given adjoining suites. Scorpio sank down on a low platform bed, his head in his hands. Leah looked around at the opulent appointments of the room. "Well, you wanted us to do better than sleeping in a doorway, and I guess you got your wish."

"Yes, these rooms are a very pleasant prison," he said. "Through the doors are locked, they'll be surprised when they find these apartments empty," said Scorpio extending the orb toward Leah. She placed her hand over it and closed her eyes as if preparing for another leap in time.

Scorpio teetered again on the lip of a great pit of darkness. Waves of gelid cold slipped over him. He felt his very existence threatened.

Leah opened her eyes and looked surprised to find herself still here.

"I c-can't," he said aloud. "You saw it, didn't you? That terrible pit of nothingness at our feet."

"I saw not-time, not-space just as I always do when the orb jumps."

"Igre's gullet!" said Scorpio suddenly.

Leah looked at him questioningly.

"The story of Igre's gullet is told by adults to naughty fry."

"Oh, a scare-babe story."

"The monster Igre may be legendary, or maybe it's something that once swam in the seas of Terrapin. At any rate it's a gigantic creature, and its gullet goes on forever. It is said that it swims around, looking for disobedient young ones, its favorite food. Then it gobbles them up. When I contemplate a jump, Igre's gullet opens up at my feet, like a black abyss."

"Scorpio, you're an adult, not a fry, and stories told by careless adults are just that—stories."

"Part of me knows that, of course. But Aquay are diffident by nature and by parental training. I was taught that aggression was wrong, that a good little fry is timid and obedient. That's the part of me that fears using the orb. I've been doing all sorts of things my people find repugnant. The reaction to this is catching up with me. So I can't face using the orb, not even to save our lives."

"It's all right," said Leah comfortingly. "I'll try to think of something."

"We're not only locked in," said Scorpio, "There's a guard posted out there. I can see him marching back and forth."

Leah sat down on a comfortable chair. "Let's give him a chance to get tired," she said.

It must have been much later when Scorpio awoke to Leah's whisper. "I think we have to try this now. They may guard us in shifts, and I don't want to take a chance that this sentry will be relieved by somebody well rested." From a corner of the room she dragged out a rattan trunk with a stout latch. "I guess this will do," she said, opening it and turning out the contents upon the floor. "Now give me the orb. Oh, and find someplace to hide that stuff." She motioned toward the trunk's contents.

Scorpio handed it over, and did as she had asked. When he returned, Leah stood by the open window. She leaned out and called to the man on watch. "Are you feeling tired? Feet hurt?"

The man was silent for a moment, a rigid silhouette. At last he growled back. "What do you think?"

"You might be interested to know that our talents include

the healing arts. Give me a minute and I'll make your feet stop hurting."

"Healing arts, my—" began the soldier, but Scorpio noticed that he walked toward the window.

"This won't take a minute," said Leah, "and you'll feel so much better. Hold out your hand."

"This better not be some trick," he said, patting his side-arm.

"No tricks," said Leah. "Do you really think that I could hurt you, or that he could?"

"No, you don't look so dangerous," said the guard, and offered his hand, palm up. "What's that?" he asked alarmed as he saw the glowing orb.

"This is our magical cure-all," said Leah putting the orb against his hand.

"It's true!" said the soldier, looking down at his feet and taking a few smart parade steps across the grass. "It is like magic. What is that thing?"

Leah shut the window.

A few minutes later, they heard the door being unlocked. "Why did you shut me out?" the guard said. "I want to know more about that magical cure-all."

"It's supposed to be kept secret," said Leah. "Lon Nol has ordered several cases of them from us for use by his medical personnel." She pointed at the trunk. "That's our sample case. It's the reason we were brought here and why we must be guarded."

"No one told me anything," he said. "A whole case of those things?" He looked at the trunk interestedly.

"Since we have so many," she said, looking at Scorpio, "perhaps it wouldn't hurt to give him just one. Open the trunk and let him pick one out."

Scorpio lifted the lid as the soldier bent over the trunk. Leah threw her whole weight behind the shove that sent him into it, and Scorpio dropped the lid and latched it. They looked at each other with satisfaction as the trunk rattled and shook and hopped across the floor with the man's exertions to escape.

"It probably won't be long until the changing of the watch," said Leah. "Let's go."

By the time they had left the grounds of Lon Nol's headquarters, it was almost dawn. At this hour they found that the streets were almost deserted. Only a few peasants trundled their carts, loaded with produce, along the street. There would be no chance of mingling with the passersby to foil pursuit. Already panting with exhaustion, Scorpio and Leah came to an intersection and looked wildly about. Looking back they could see the guards of Lon Nol gaining ground rapidly.

"I wish I'd had more time to explore the city," said Leah. "All this is unfamiliar to me." They chose a direction at random and ran on, but not knowing the area, Leah, who had learned some skills in evading pursuers, could find no place for them to hide.

At last they could go no further, and pausing before a narrow opening between two buildings, darted inside. It was so dark that Scorpio could hardly see a thing. It was only by touch that he discovered the passageway ended with a wall of damp stone.

"We've got to go back," said Leah frantically. In the darkness they collided with each other, and before they could reach the entrance again, they heard running footsteps and harsh voices.

"They went in there!"

"We've got them now!"

"We might as well give ourselves up," said Scorpio. Then

a shiver went through him as he felt a tiny hand clasp his, and he heard a whisper.

"Come with me."

He allowed himself to be led into an opening so small he had to bend almost double to enter it. His feet splashed in water as he walked. "Leah?" he said, his voice echoing in the confined space.

"Yes, I'm here."

"Be silent," came a peremptory though high-pitched voice. They seemed to walk for a long time, and finally Scorpio, feeling wet and bedraggled, came blinking into daylight out of the mouth of a large storm drain. He looked down and saw the boy he had rescued from the angry merchant.

Behind them Leah was being led by two other children. It was difficult to tell their sex because of the sameness of their pajama-like garments, the dirt on their faces and their raggedly cut hair.

"This is not a situation for children," said Leah.

"Why did you rescue us?" asked Scorpio.

"Because you helped me," said the boy. "Honor is not a small thing to a Khmer. I am Chi, and these are my friends, Siv and Khieu."

Now that the immediate danger was over, the three children gathered together and talked, solemn-faced, like old men in council.

"They are safe now," said Siv. "We can let them make their way."

"They are not safe," said Chi. "The soldiers will be everywhere in the city. We must take them home with us."

"We took a pledge not to divulge our hideout, remember? said Siv. "And I don't like the way the tall one looks. Like a *naga*. Besides, Jonnie-Lo would be very angry."

"Yes," said Chi, thoughtfully. After a long pause he added, "Then he will have to be angry. My honor is more important."

They argued for some moments until Chi finally convinced them. "You are to come with us," said Chi approaching Leah and Scorpio.

"You are only babies," said Leah. "Where are your parents? Where are those who care for you?"

Siv and Khieu looked at her silently, stolid looks on their faces, but a certain remembrance came into their eyes when she mentioned parents.

"We have no parents," said Chi almost matter-of-factly. "And we care for ourselves. You may go with us, or stay here. But the soldiers will probably be along soon, unless they got lost in the drains."

Siv and Khieu giggled at this.

"They know the hiding places and we don't," said Scorpio.

"All right," said Leah exasperatedly.

Chapter
3

*T*hey made their way along
the edge of the city until they reached an area of abandoned
structures. A bridge had collapsed into a stream, and by a
circuitous path the children led them under a portion of the
bridge still standing. Makeshift walls had been created by
leaning sheets of tin and cardboard against the bridge's sup-
ports. As they entered the hideout, they saw two more children chasing each other about the dim interior. One that
could have been no more than five or six years old, clasped a
filthy and ragged doll.

Leah was appalled to see the place they lived. The floor
was of hard-packed earth, and debris had gathered in all the
corners. She thought Chi, who had ordered them about like a
miniature general, sounded deferential and a little afraid
when he asked, "Where is Jonnie-Lo?"

"I don't know," said the littlest one. "He went out. Why
did you bring these grown-ups here? Why does that one look
so funny, like a *rakshasa*?"

"My friend is not a demon," said Leah to the small child.
She supposed she was a girl because of the ragged doll she

27

clutched. "Scorpio, I can't believe that all these children live here, under this bridge, like—like barbarians."

"Obviously, they do," said Scorpio. "If you've lost your parents, isn't there someone in the city who would take you in?" he asked Chi.

"Some of us came from the orphanage," he said, "but with the war, there were too many to care for and they ran out of money. I didn't like it there anyway, and Jonnie-Lo found us and helped us make this hideout."

"He taught us how to get our food from the merchants, too," said Siv. "It's real easy. One of us creates a disturbance, and the others fill their pockets and sacks."

"You mean you steal your food," said Leah. "That's terrible."

"Then I guess you won't want anything to eat," said Khieu, taking fruit from a sack as the others gathered around.

"I saved you some," said Scorpio later as he returned to the corner that Leah had staked out for them. In that area she had already made headway against the trash that cluttered every inch of the hideout.

She stopped her work and sat down on a box to eat what he had brought. She ate around some brown spots on the bananas and wondered if the children hadn't been exaggerating their thieving prowess. When fruit spoiled, the merchants threw it out. "We still have some money, don't we?" she asked.

"Yes, but I don't think we'll be able to go back into the fortune-telling business, so we'll have to be sparing with it."

"Tomorrow we'll buy some rice. Maybe some fish. I wonder how long it's been since these children had a hot meal. Or for that matter, a bath." She looked at their grimy clothing and smeared faces. "I don't suppose there's any water about."

"The stream beyond this bridge still flows, if it's not too full of sewage or factory wastes." Scorpio grimaced. It was almost blasphemy to him to see rivers and lakes polluted by the people who lived near them.

They went down to the water's edge. Chunks of iron and concrete from the fallen bridge lay in the water like immense stepping stones. Scorpio leaned down; his nostrils twitched. "It's not as clear as the waters of Terrapin, but for an earth stream, it's not bad."

By this time Chi and others had seen Leah and Scorpio by the water, and curiosity caused them to gather around. "Come here," urged Leah. "I've been thinking that what you need is a nice bath. Wouldn't you like that?" She had no soap for them to wash with, but even water was a good beginning.

There was a general moaning and groaning. "What do you think you are, our *Ma*?" said Chi. The rest laughed.

Without a word Scorpio sat on the muddy bank and slid into the water, amid general uproar from the children. He dived deep and then broke the surface, spouting water from his mouth, exactly as he used to do among his friends on Terrapin.

Scant seconds later the children were sliding down the bank. There was diving and splashing in imitation of Scorpio. Leah sighed. It hadn't been what she had had in mind, but the effect would be the same.

She returned to the hideout to find what she could in the way of dry clothes for when they came out.

Later that evening, she sat with Vanna, the youngest, who had fallen asleep on her lap. Phal, the other boy, looked up at her at the sound of angry voices outside. Gently putting the child down, she went to the doorway.

A threatening figure stood over Chi. He was only a silhouette in the gathering dusk, but his shape was distinct with menace. Jonnie-Lo.

"*You* decided to bring strangers into out midst?" said Jonnie-Lo. "SInce when do any of you decide anything? I protected you, taught you to survive. I demand your obedience in all things."

"It was a matter of my . . . honor," said Chi, saying the final word in a small voice without conviction. "Scorpio saved my life so I owed—"

"Did you ever consider that they might betray us to the authorities? You know that grown people have odd beliefs. One of them is that children can't live on their own, that they're better off in orphanages."

"I didn't think—" began Chi, his voice breaking.

Leah saw that Scorpio was edging closer to the confrontation, as if not sure that he should intervene. She joined him. As she drew closer, she saw that Jonnie-Lo could only be a few years older than Chi, but he had a thin, feral face and whipcord body. It wouldn't be so hard to picture him behind a rifle. Leah had seen many soldiers who were barely more than boys.

"The intruders will have to leave," said Jonnie-Lo, "and I'm afraid, since you were responsible, I'll have to punish you." Jonnie-Lo reached over to a nearby tree and broke off a branch.

"No," shouted Leah, running up to them. "Leave him alone."

"You have no business being here," said Jonnie-Lo, "and interfering between me and my friends." He raised the branch again, but this time it was aimed at Leah.

She turned her face aside in anticipation of the blow, but it never fell. When she looked again, she saw that Scorpio had overcome his reserve and had grasped Jonnie-Lo by the wrist. Scorpio had approached out of darkness, so the bully hadn't realized he was anything but a normal man. Jonnie-Lo struggled a moment as he felt someone grab him, but his eyes went wide as he saw the slightly webbed fingers with their gray skin. When he looked up into Scorpio's face, he shrieked and dropped the branch.

"What are you? Please, please let me go," he pleaded, his legs going out from under him, leaving him kneeling in the dirt. Scorpio looked surprised at the reaction, and Leah knew that in a moment Scorpio would release him and it would be obvious the tall alien could harm no one. Then they would have Jonnie-Lo to contend with again.

"Scorpio, please let him go," said Leah. "It's not as if you're all that hungry. You finished off one of these children at dinnertime."

Hearing this, Jonnie-Lo gave an extra effort and jerked himself free. His feet scrambled in the loose dirt a moment before momentum sent him careening off into the brush.

"He didn't hurt you, did he?" Leah asked Chi.

"No," said Chi, looking very sad.

"What's the matter? I don't think he'll be back."

"That's the problem. Jonnie-Lo was cruel sometimes, but I think he was right that we can't survive without him."

Leah put her arm around Chi's shoulder, feeling him shivering in the coolness of the evening. "It'll be all right," she assured him, though considering that she and Scorpio were both on the run, she wasn't terribly sure herself. She hadn't thought about it before, but she supposed it was the kind of wishful promise parents always gave their children in an uncertain world.

Several days later Leah and Scorpio stood and looked at their work. The hideout had been totally cleaned of debris, and pieces of tin and cardboard had been fond to make it more secure against rain and wind. "This is a great improvement," said Scorpio.

"Yes," sighed Leah, "but it's still just a space under a bridge with a bare dirt floor. And our money will soon run out. I don't want to have to see the children return to stealing, or even scavenging their food. There must be some authorities in the city who make provisions for orphans."

"Chi told us his orphanage closed down," said Scorpio.

"I know, but maybe there are other institutions, or maybe some family would take them in."

"But no one even knows about them."

"Of course, a newspaper!" said Leah excitedly. "If the word were sent out that these children need homes, there's a chance that kind-hearted volunteers would come forward. You remember that restaurant, the one where they said all the reporters gathered?"

"I don't know; they looked awfully preoccupied talking among themselves. How do you know they'd even listen to you?"

Leah reached into her pocket and dug around. At last she came up with a stained and creased bit of paper. "My press pass from the old Russian paper, the *Narodny Slovo*. I'll mingle with the reporters, and when the time is right, make my request."

Leah paused before entering the restaurant, and looked down at her new clothes. On her first visit she had noticed that those inside didn't dress like the peasants and poor people she had come in contact with, so she had stopped in a store to change the way she looked. She didn't want to be conspicuous. Some of the male correspondents wore the jacket, pants and decorative strip of material hanging down under their chins that had so amused Scorpio, and some of the women were dressed practically like the men.

Leah had chosen a dark blue skirt and jacket. The skirt was scandalously short, and when the shopgirl had shown her the pantyhose she was to wear with it, she had begun to laugh helplessly. The garment not only looked ridiculous, it was so sheer she might as well have gone bare-legged. *I'm glad Grandmere Zarah can't see me in this outfit,* she thought.

No one looked up as she entered; they were too involved in their conversations. She supposed that meant her disguise was working. She sat down at a table and tried to listen in on what was being said, but the place was so small and so crowded, she didn't have much luck. The waiter came and she ordered a cup of tea.

She had almost drunk it all when a man and a woman came in quickly and looked around for a place to sit.

"You don't mind, do you, love?" asked the man, pulling out an empty chair at Leah's table. He looked youngish with his curly red hair and freckles, but wasn't all that young. "C'mon Roz."

The woman with him hesitated. She was tall and angular with a sunburned, peeling face. There was something open about her expression that made Leah trust her. "Sorry," she said. "Ian never minds foisting himself off on someone."

"I don't mind," said Leah. "I was alone anyway."

Even after the two of them had sat down, Leah still felt like an outsider, because they continued a conversation that must have begun much earlier. Only when the subject changed did she feel on familiar ground. She realized they were discussing the war and the impending invasion.

"Lon Nol told me that without a miracle Angka will take the city within a month," she said, and the two others fell instantly silent.

"You interviewed Lon Nol?" asked Roz.

"*The* Lon Nol?" asked Ian flippantly, in a way that conveyed his doubt.

"Certainly. He's a squat, somewhat ugly man, very dark—"

"She's interviewed Lon Nol," said Roz.

"She's *seen* him anyway," said Ian.

"What paper are you with?" asked Roz. "I don't believe I've seen you around here before."

Nervously Leah produced the press pass.

"Never heard of it," said Ian.

"I suppose you'd know all about the press in the USSR," said Roz.

The reporters seemed properly impressed. Leah considered how she might work the news about the children's plight into the conversation.

"Oh, did you get your film developed? I was wanting to see how those shots you took came out," asked Roz.

Ian reached into a leather bag and took out a sheaf of paper squares. Leah's eyes widened as she saw that each square of paper held the miniature of what looked like a real scene, precise as a reflection in clear water: a view of the street with its varied traffic, one of the ornate buildings called pagodas, the sight of loitering soldiers. She bit back the urge to ask, "How did you do that?" since she was pretending to be from this time period. Roz was shuffling through the scenes, as if there were nothing of black magic in a true representation of real things, only smaller.

As Roz lined up the photographs on the tabletop, Leah's gaze was sharply arrested for the second time, and she felt a sudden thrill of fear. *How easy it is to make a new home, to begin to feel safe,* she thought, *without being safe at all.*

Involuntarily, Leah reached out and picked up the photo.

"That's a really odd one," said Ian. "I can't remember taking it. The guy must have wandered into my field of view without my knowing it."

"Now that you mention it, it is," said Roz. The scene showed a tall, slim humanoid figure with skin as red and shiny as lacquer. The lower part of his face ended in a beaklike arrangement, which would have looked alien to Leah, except that Scorpio's face was similar. The creature wore a flowing black robe and what appeared to be a cap with ram's horns curling to either side of his head.

"Well, now what do you suppose this guy is tricked out for? Halloween?" said Roz.

The Hunter, thought Leah, *he followed us here. He's in the city, stalking us.*

"Some religious pageant, I suppose," said Ian. "Or maybe a ballet. These people are crazy about dance. They're always recreating the old legends with masks and costumes."

Roz squinted closely at the picture. "Yes, that's what it has to be, but it's a very effective costume. Looks almost real, doesn't it?"

Leah pushed her chair back hastily. "I'm sorry," she blurted out. "I have to go. I forgot an appointment." She rushed out, leaving Ian and Roz staring puzzledly after her.

I've got to tell Scorpio, she thought, racing frantically through the streets.

When she reached the hideout, she saw Scorpio sitting on a crate with children crowded around him. "I've got to talk to you," she said.

"*Ta* Scorpio was telling us about the games children play on Aquay," said Siv. Chi had teasingly begun calling Leah and Scorpio *Ma* and *Ta*, mother and father, and it had caught on.

"This is important," said Leah.

Scorpio lifted Vanna down off his lap and disengaged himself from clinging arms.

"The Hunter is here," she said as soon as they were out of the children's hearing range.

"Lethor, here? Have you seen him?"

"Only in a manner of speaking," said Leah, remembering the magical images with a shiver. "I do know that he's here, and he can have but one purpose—to find us."

"By some misunderstanding he thinks I killed his companion. If I could just explain—"

"Scorpio, his mission was to kill us even before his companion Ardon managed to get himself killed. What good would explanations possibly do?"

"I would feel better," said Scorpio.

Leah made a muffled sound of frustration. "I can't figure out how he's able to find us no matter where in time we go."

"Even when we don't know where we're going."

"The orb knows, though. Do you suppose that's it? One orb tracking another?"

"Then he's sure to find us," said Scorpio, "and I can't even use the orb to escape."

"He hasn't found us yet, even though he must have been here several days. Maybe his orb can't locate ours when it's not being used."

"He might find us anyway. My fortune-telling business gave us a certain notoriety in the city. And we can't run. Who would care for the children?"

"So what do we do?" asked Leah.

"I guess we just have to wait."

Chapter
4

*A*ngry at herself that she had forgotten the children's plight when she saw the Hunter was in Phnom Penh, Leah returned to the restaurant every day, but Roz and Ian weren't there.

She was on her way there again, when she noticed that the streets were almost deserted. For weeks there had been nothing but talk about the advancing army. She hurried, feeling something of the nervousness that pervaded the city, and this time she was rewarded by the sight of Roz and Ian at their usual table.

"What do you hear from Lon Nol?" said Ian as she entered.

"Shut up, Ian," said Roz.

"I expect he's sweating plenty by now, if he hasn't already made a run for it. After all, the Khmer Rouge are practically knocking at his door."

"I could tell something was up," said Leah, "by the way the people talk. Some of them think a takeover by Angka will be an improvement over the corrupt government they have now. Some of them are just scared."

"I don't blame them," said Roz, "after all, nobody knows

anything about the Khmer Rouge or what plans they have for the country if they win."

"Anyway, I'm working on another story now," said Leah. "Did you know that in this city children are forced to live like animals, stealing their food and taking shelter where they can?"

Ian looked surprised, as if in covering his stories of war he had never taken into account the suffering that went along with it. *Of course, maybe he can't,* thought Leah, *not and still do his job.*

"I think we do know," said Roz, "in a sort of objective way, but it sounds as if you have the inside story."

"I—and a friend—we're taking care of some children we found living under a bridge. I thought that if people knew about them, their own people might take them in and give them a proper home."

"Maybe some sort of notice could be put in a local paper," said Roz, "but we don't know—"

"We can talk to the editors of the local papers," said Ian curtly. "I don't know if it'll do any good considering that the city's under siege, but we can still try."

"Thanks." She turned to go.

"Wait, where can we find you if we're able to help?"

"I'll come here every day," said Leah.

Several more days passed with no word from the reporters. Leah awoke one morning to the sound of rumbling trucks and loudspeakers telling the people to come out into the streets.

Warning the children to stay inside, Leah and Scorpio joined a group of people moving toward the sounds. "They're here," someone said. "The Khmer Rouge. They've finally taken the city."

The message the loudspeaker was broadcasting sounded

simple: *Everyone must evacuate the city immediately because of the danger of bombing by the American devils. Go to your home villages, or the villages of your grandfathers. Leave your property; escape with your lives.*

"Bombing," said a passerby. "Do you think there really is a danger?"

"Perhaps not," said someone else, "but we'll have to take their word for it." He indicated a troop of black-pajama-clad soldiers working their way down the street, making sure that all the people had left their homes to hear the message.

"If I just had the courage to use the orb—" said Scorpio.

"It makes no difference. Neither of us could leave the children now. Our place is here, no matter how unlikely that seems."

Leah was startled as Scorpio grabbed her around the waist and swung her around behind him. She saw that he had pulled her out of the way of a group of black-clad soldiers who had just run by. "At least we'll probably lose Lethor in the confusion. Let's go back and get the children."

When they returned to the hideout, the children clustered around them as Leah explained what had happened.

"But this is our home," wailed Vanna clutching her doll closer. "Why can't we stay?"

Leah looked around the makeshift shelter that she had worked so hard to clean. It would never be a proper home, yet she knew that she, too, would miss it and the moments she and Scorpio had shared with the children.

"We have to go because there may be danger here. Or at least that's what we were told. Do any of you know the name of your home village or that of your relatives?"

Five faces looked blank.

"Well, then we can go where we like," said Scorpio. "Gather up your possessions. We're lucky that we can take almost everything we own with us. Some people will probably have to leave a lot behind."

Leah smiled in spite of herself. Only an Aquay would make a virtue of poverty.

A few minutes later, their possessions in bundles on their backs or under their arms, the unlikely family moved out into the streets where anonymous crowds streamed from the city like ants from a crushed anthill.

Troops of Khmer Rouge moved here and there throughout the city, overseeing the exodus and keeping everyone moving.

"Hang onto each other and me or Scorpio," Leah cautioned the children as they negotiated a crowded street. Drivers of motor vehicles leaned on their horns, adding to the confusion as they tried to work their way through the throngs of refugees.

As they reached the city's edge, they saw several huge trucks lined up by the side of the road. Officials with clipboards were directing people into the trucks.

"Is your village to the north?" shouted one of them, his voice almost lost in the rumble of engines.

"We don't have a home village," said Leah. The man looked at her sharply, shaking his head, though she didn't know why he was looking at her and Scorpio so disapprovingly, unless it was because they were obviously so different from the children who clung to them.

"Then get in here," he said, indicating a truck.

Leah wasn't so sure she liked the idea, since the truck was already crowded with people. Scorpio shrugged and began to lift the children in one by one. Once on board they elbowed their way to an unoccupied spot. The truck took off with a roar, throwing up a cloud of dust.

Swaying with the mass of bodies crammed into the truck bed, Leah tried to make some sense of the landscape sliding by. That glint of blue-gray parallel to the road must be the Mekong River. As they traveled further into the countryside, they saw green rice paddies and peasants' houses set on pilings, out of the way of seasonal flooding.

"Do you know where they're taking us?" she asked a woman beside her.

"They said we would go to a cooperative and learn a new way of life," said the woman.

"Well, maybe it won't be so bad if it means a good home for the children," said Leah.

Later they stopped at a sort of way station where the people lined up for food, but the food ran out before the line had gotten halfway through.

"We still have some of our own," said Scorpio opening his bundle.

"I'm not so sure about this," said Leah. "They haven't planned well if they brought us out here without any means to keep us fed."

To get out of the heat of the afternoon sun, they went under some trees to eat their meal. The others quickly fell asleep after they had eaten from the exhaustion of the trip, but Leah felt restless. She decided to walk around until she, too, felt sleepy. As she strolled past the way station, she heard voices from inside. Glancing in at the window, she noticed that one of the speakers was the bureaucrat with a clipboard who had directed them to board the truck. Suspicion about the journey made her crouch down and approach the window so she could hear what was being said.

"I noticed a few foreigners in this load," one of them was saying.

"We'll leave them off when we stop at Siem Reap," said the other. "They'll be sent to a re-education camp. Only people of pure Khmer blood are wanted at the cooperatives. That's one of the goals: to weed out the undesirables."

Stealthily, Leah crept away from the window and made her way back to where Scorpio and the others were still sleeping. "Wake up," she said urgently, shaking Scorpio.

He roused groggily. "What is it?"

"I've just heard that we're not to be allowed to go with the children to the cooperative. We're to be sent to some other camp."

"We can't let them go without us," said Scorpio. "Who'd look out for them?"

"That's what I decided," said Leah, "so that's why we have to slip away now."

Scorpio looked around. Encroaching at the edges of the clearing was thickly grown jungle, immense trees hung with ropy vines.

"Doesn't it look a little wild?"

"Yes, but I think this will be our last chance to act if we don't want to be separated from the children." She looked back toward the way station. Several black-clad soldiers had gathered there, and they seemed to be playing some kind of game of chance. Their attention was on something in the middle of the circle they formed, not on the refugees. But she was certain that if she and Scorpio weren't cautious, the guards would remember their duties.

One by one she awakened the children, whispering what she planned to each one in turn. Vanna went first, toddling about in the field as if in pursuit of a butterfly. When she reached the jungle's edge, she disappeared behind the bole of a tree. Leah breathed a sigh of relief to see her go. She looked back at the guards, and seeing that they were still occupied, signalled to Phal.

The game of chance began to break up, and Leah, Scorpio and Chi still remained to make their escape. "We can't wait any longer," Leah whispered. "We have to make a run for it. Now!" They began to run, each of them making for a different part of the jungle to try and confuse any pursuit. Leah heard the whine and impact of a gunshot, but she was running too hard to know if she was actually being fired at. Another bullet ploughed up the dirt almost under her feet, and this time she knew that she had been the target.

The jungle's oppressive dampness closed around her, and she had to fight her way free of a tangle of vines. She began to wonder if her idea was such a good one, now that she was actually here. She had difficulty finding her way and wondered if she could locate any of the others.

Then in the green gloom she saw Vanna crouched between the enormous twisting roots of a tree. Leah gathered her up and whispered, "We've got to go deeper in case they come after us. I hope we can find the others somehow."

Looking over her shoulder to see if she was being tracked by the guards, Leah carried Vanna deeper into the jungle. She stopped, hardly breathing, as she heard a rustling in the undergrowth. Scorpio and Phal came out of a thicket, hand in hand. Leah and Vanna rushed to greet them.

"What if Chi and the others got lost?" asked Vanna.

"Then we'll find them, somehow," said Scorpio. "We're a family, and families stick together."

Leah wasn't so sure they'd ever see the others again. Immense mosquitoes landed on her face and hands, and thorns caught at her clothes. Once, when she reached out to grasp a branch to steady herself, what she had thought was a ropy vine began to slide under her hand. The snake, perfectly camouflaged for a place of light and shadow by the patterns on its body, slithered higher on the branch. She yelled, drawing everyone's attention, and then wished she had been able to muffle the sound. Pursuers might hear it, too.

"Can't we stop?" asked Phal.

"We will soon, but we have to be sure we're not being followed." As she spoke, Scorpio whirled around.

"I heard something."

They hid behind a screen of brush and waited until anxiety became an ache. After a moment, Chi, Siv and Khieu appeared, clothes torn and faces dirty. All of them gathered together with cries of delight, no longer worrying about pursuit. It was like a miracle to Leah that in the jungle's dank gloom somehow they'd all found each other again. The jungle no longer seemed so alien to her. It didn't matter where they were; as long as they were all together, things really would be all right.

"I smell water," said Scorpio. "Lots of it!"

They climbed a hill going in the direction Scorpio pointed and after awhile they emerged from the jungle's darkness to see a huge expanse of water spread before them, blue as a jewel against the surrounding green.

"I've heard of that," said Chi. "Tonle Sap, the Great Lake."

"More like an inland sea," said Scorpio. "Let's journey toward it—I'd like a swim."

"We need to begin thinking about some sort of shelter for the night," Leah said. She thought about the snake and shuddered, not wanting to spend the night on the bare ground or even in a tree where snakes or insects could come and go at will.

"I'm not sure we can count on a real shelter," said Scorpio, "but there may be a cave or the overhang of a ledge to spend the night in."

They traveled on. A little further into the jungle, they came upon the wreckage of some vehicle, the metal twisted and warped almost out of all recognition. The fire that had consumed it had made a little space for itself, but the jungle growth was returning quickly with fresh green shoots. The children looked at it curiously as they passed. Leah supposed it was a military vehicle of some sort, letting them know that the war had passed this way, despite the thickness of the growth.

It was late afternoon. The little band was almost ready to make camp right on the spot. Leah was so exhausted she had forgotten all about the snake, and even the detritus of the forest floor looked inviting. Chi had stopped ahead of them, peering upward.

"What's wrong?" asked Scorpio.

"I saw a face."

"A face. Is someone sneaking up on us?" said Leah.

"I don't think so. This is a big face. Look."

Leah looked through a gap in the canopy of leaves overhead and was startled to see that Chi was right. An immense stone face was framed by the opening in the trees.

"Who would build a statue in the middle of the wilderness?" asked Leah.

"Those are the old places," said Siv. "The ruins of our ancestors from a time when the Khmers ruled the world. I've seen some of the statues and artifacts in the museum."

"Some of the ruins have been restored," said Chi, "but there were so many that the government just left some of them to be overgrown by jungle."

"Maybe we've found our shelter," said Leah moving off in the direction of the stone face.

Light descending through the many-layered canopy of leaves was green and indistinct. Shadows moved with each gust of wind. Leah had the feeling of walking on a seafloor as she walked among the ruins. Time and jungle growth had created a different sort of effect than the builders had ever intended.

Great crumbling towers wore crowns of shrubs and saplings, and thick tree roots grasped immense blocks of hewn stone like the tentacles of a mysterious sea creature. Many of the antique structures had weathered away to smoothness, but here and there carvings stood out in relief. Leah stopped to study the carving of a beautiful young woman set into a niche in the wall.

"That is an *apsara*," said Siv, putting her own hands in the position of those of the woman in the carving. "A celestial dancer chosen to entertain the gods."

Leah looked at the carving. The dancer was dressed in an ornate headdress, earrings, necklaces and bracelets, with an intricate wrapped skirt completing the costume. Before her time traveling, she would have thought it only an interesting work of art. Now she knew it could be the representation of a real person separated by the thin barrier of a thousand years. The play of light and shadow made the dancer appear to sway.

They moved on, exploring as much of the ruins as they could.

"Looks like we have the place all to ourselves," said Scorpio. As he leaned over to inspect a carving of a winged creature of some sort, a projectile bounced off his shoulder and he jumped back. "Get down!" he ordered. "Maybe we were followed."

Leah and the children took cover just as a barrage of nutshells, twigs and other debris descended from the branches above. First Chi, and then the other children, started laughing and pointing to the troop of monkeys that had them pinned down.

To Leah, who was unfamiliar with these animals, they looked uncomfortably like small, furry human beings as they crouched in the branches looking down at the intruders. Then they would extend long arms and legs and become all animal as they made their way nimbly through the treetops.

Chi stood up, picked up a nutshell, and cast it back. He was rewarded with another rain of debris from above. When everyone else came out from cover, the big, gray-furred monkey who seemed to be the leader, screeched in frustration and fear, and breaking ranks, the monkey troop went scattering in all directions.

"I think that big gray-furred one must have been Sugriva, the prince of monkeys," said Siv.

"Don't be a baby, this isn't some old story," said Chi.

Birds of bright colors rose flapping and squawking from nests among the masonry as Leah and the others passed. Earlier she had been ready to lie down and sleep on the jungle floor; now she had become more particular, with the remains of an entire city to choose from. She found a structure almost intact and peered in through one of the doorways. "Your ancestors certainly lived on a grand scale," said Leah, looking at the large chamber.

"They didn't live in these monuments," said Khieu, impatiently, as if she thought everyone ought to know. "These were the temples and tombs. The people, even the kings, lived in houses of wood nearby. Only the structures of stone survived."

"This looks like it would work," said Scorpio, putting down the bundle of possessions he was still carrying.

"At ground level here we could still be sharing our bed with the insects and animals that wandered in," she said. "Look, I believe those stairs lead up into a tower."

She began to negotiate the stairway, and though several steps had crumbled away and the path was choked with sticks, leaves and other debris, she made her way upward.

Before she arrived, she began to smell a sharp odor, and there was a faint rustling sound. When she looked into the tower room, she saw what looked like several fat gray chrysalides dangling from the ceiling. "What—" she began, and the rustling noise grew to a roar as the bat colony began to take to the air. Brown wings thrashed and furry bodies careened about, before making an escape through windows and openings in the tower.

Leah turned and bolted down the stairs, not realizing that Phal, Chi and Scorpio had followed her up. They collided and stumbled the rest of the way down.

"I guess we'll be all right down here for tonight after all," said Leah. "By the smell, the tower has been occupied for some time. I guess we'll have to learn to share our new home."

The next few days were busy as they explored the ruins further. The building where they had spent the night was one of the few structures standing intact, so they decided to make that their home. Gathering some green wood, they built a smoky fire at the foot of the staircase and then ran outside. An endless stream of bats shot from windows and openings in the tower wall.

"After all, why should bats have the best room in the house?" said Leah. "We'll weave some rattan into coverings for the windows and caulk the openings with mud, but first we'd better go out foraging for some food. I noticed some coconut palms on our way here."

Leah noticed that Siv wasn't paying any attention to her. She was simply staring off into space as if lost in her own thoughts. Of course, that was fairly typical of Siv, but Leah wanted everyone's attention. There was work to be done.

She sent the rest ahead and turned to Siv. "You seem distracted this morning. Didn't you sleep well?"

"*Ma* Leah, must we stay in this awful place?" said Siv, tears beginning to course down her cheeks.

"I know it looks rough now," said Leah, "but in a few days it'll be more snug than the old hideout. We can be happy here, you'll see."

"Last night, I must have walked in my sleep as I often do,

and I awoke to find myself outside. Just as I was about to return to my sleeping place, I saw her."

"Who did you see?"

"The *apsara* from the wall. It must have been she, for she was crowned with a headdress of gold and precious gems that glittered in the moonlight as she moved. She danced so—oh, it was beautiful, but it was frightening, too. How can a thing of stone dance across the grass as light as air? Even though I was frightened, I called out to her, but she danced on. Not only did she not hear me, I had the feeling she couldn't see me, either. I don't think I want to live in a haunted place."

Leah put her arm around Siv and drew her close. "The simplest explanation is usually the best. Didn't you say that you were sleepwalking before you saw the dancer? What if she were only part of your dream and you confused waking and sleeping?"

Siv looked a little comforted, so Leah suggested they join the others. Soon Siv was running along the jungle paths with her friends as if she had forgotten the experience. *She's so sensitive,* Leah thought. *If there are ghosts about, she'd be the one to see them. And what would an ancient ruin like this be without a few wandering spirits? We're certainly safer here than we were in Phnom Penh.* She couldn't help wondering what was happening in the city and about the fate of the people in the trucks. *At least we're safe here.*

"We may get a little sick of fruit and coconuts," said Leah, as they foraged about under the trees.

"I'll be glad to make a trip to the Tonle Sap later on," offered Scorpio. "We can add fish and perhaps shellfish to our diet."

The children began to clamor to be the one to accompany him.

"And maybe you'll even find time to splash about in the water."

"Maybe I will at that."

"Look out!" cried Leah, as she saw Scorpio stumble as if he'd caught his foot on something. A huge log that had been propped up overhead was hurtling downward. Leah put both hands on Scorpio's back and pushed as hard as she could, barely scrambling out of the way as the log slammed into the earth.

"A deadfall," said Scorpio, picking himself up and coming back to inspect the device. His foot had caught on a trip wire that had sent the log crashing down. "I'm afraid we'll have to be a little more careful as we wander about. We can't forget that at some point this jungle was a battleground. All sorts of traps could have been left."

Chapter 5

*C*han watched his men fan out as they moved through the jungle. He had warned them to step cautiously to avoid any traps or mines that might have been left from battles fought here. Green gloom under the trees almost swallowed them up. Here and there he caught a glimpse of the red checkered scarves worn as headbands which had become an insignia for the Khmer Rouge. He was young for a leader, just seventeen, but he had advanced rapidly after being recruited by the Communist Youth Corps. There was opportunity for the young because old leaders who had cooperated with the Lon Nol regime were no longer trusted.

Trang, who had been a boyhood friend, fell into step with him. "Do you think it's true what they said about this foreigner we're looking for?" he asked. "Could he be some sort of monster?"

"Don't think like a peasant," said Chan.

"That's hard," said Trang, "since that's what we are."

"Maybe you don't have any more ambition than that," said Chan, "but that's why we have formulated the 'great

51

leap forward' to bring Democratic Kampuchea into the twentieth century in just one generation."

"Oh it's 'we' is it?" said Trang. "Have you risen so high that the leaders have taken you into their confidence?"

Chan knew his friend was only poking fun at Chan's new, responsible attitude. For a moment he felt an impulse to leap at Trang and wrestle him playfully to the ground as he might have done some years ago, both of them laughing. Now he only looked at him coolly. "I say 'we' because the will of the Khmers must be as one if we're to create the new, progressive state."

Trang looked crestfallen at the rebuff. Chan felt a pang of regret, then suppressed it. He was no longer the son of a poor rice farmer, with no more future than to break his back in the paddies. Maybe Trang wanted to recapture old days, but Chan had put them behind him.

"Better take your position," said Chan. "These foreigners may be harmless, but we can't be sure. We know they carried off several Khmer children into the jungle, perhaps as hostages."

Trang lowered his head briefly in deference. "Yes, sir," he muttered, and trotted off.

I can't allow old friendships to get in the way of completing this mission successfully, he told himself. *It should be routine enough, but the foreigners might be spies. I have to do well. My superiors will be watching, and they give no second chances.*

A little later, one of his men called to him. The soldier stood looking down at something on the bank of a stream. "Footprints," he said as Chan approached. "They've been by here."

Chan ordered his men to scatter through the jungle again and try to find the direction his quarry had gone. Soon, a man shouted that he had spotted a bit of cloth clinging to a thorn bush.

Toward evening they reached the ruins. Impressively ornate towers and walls of red laterite glowed balefully in the rays of sunset filtering down through the trees. Chan's men had fallen silent as they began to walk through these monuments of Cambodia's former greatness. These ruins were a familiar part of everyone's heritage, of course, but that pervasive peasant mentality was still awed by these cyclopian structures.

They'll soon start to see ancestral ghosts or something equally ridiculous, thought Chan, *unless I keep them busy.*

"Search these ruins for any sign of the refugees," he ordered, "but be careful. They may be armed."

"No one's here," said Trang, reporting back. "but we found their gear in that building." He pointed. "It looks like they established camp here and then went off someplace."

"Then we must make camp here for the night ourselves. They may come back, and it would be foolish to flounder around in the jungle after dark."

"Make camp here . . . sir?" He added the last word like an afterthought. "The men—"

"We won't create Democratic Kampuchea if we remain superstitious peasants." He turned to shout at his squad. "Fall out. We camp here tonight. Draw lots for first watch."

The men fell silent again, but he didn't hear any grumbling, so he unrolled his own sleeping bag in the shelter of what must once have been a huge gate. A line of elephants and their mahouts had been carved on one wall. *We have toiled in the shadow of these ruins long enough,* he told himself. *Now we will again build a civilization that men will marvel at.*

Except for the far-off hooting of an owl, the ruins were silent. He was soon asleep.

• • •

Chan felt anonymous in the crowds that thronged the temple gate. "Are they coming?" asked someone beside him. "Can you see anything?"

Chan heard the clatter of horses' hooves over the paving and saw cavalry leading the way, the horses with bells and garlands of flowers on their bridles. Behind them came the standard bearers and musicians, filling the air with the brightness of flags whipping in the wind and the richness of music. He was stirred, despite the fact that he didn't know where he was or how he had gotten there.

Next came a mass of palace girls, the most beautiful girls in the kingdom, wearing their most ornate headdresses and flowered sarongs. They carried the royal utensils of gold and silver.

Behind them came another troop of palace girls, though these marched in ranks and carried lances and shields with the royal crest. They were the sovereign's private guard. Chan thought he should find it strange to see these armed women serving as bodyguards, but the idea had a familiar feel.

Next came goat carts and horse carriages, decorated in gold, and behind them elephants, patiently shuffling, which carried the minsters and high-ranking officers of the court. They were awash in a veritable sea of red parasols carried by their servants.

"Ah, there she is!" shouted someone behind him, and he saw a white elephant, its trappings all of gold. On its back stood a slim girl holding aloft a golden sword, the *Preah Khan*, symbol of rule.

"The queen, the queen!" cries came from all around him, and the onlookers began to bow down, some of them falling prostrate on the pavement.

Chan could not even bow his head. His attention was held

by the beauty of the queen, though she seemed less like a queen to him than just a beautiful girl, perhaps the most beautiful he had ever seen in his life. As the elephant passed, he had the feeling that he could be in danger by not bowing. Armed cavalrymen rode beside the queen, gesturing aggressively with their swords.

Somehow no one challenged him.

The queen even looked in his direction and smiled, just as the procession passed by. Of course, she might only have been smiling at the brightness of the day or the sight of so many loyal subjects. Chan, however, couldn't shake the feeling that her smile had been for him alone.

Wakening alone in the ruins just before dawn, Chan could still almost hear the strains of the harps, the clacking of cymbals. *She was a dream,* he thought with an intense feeling of loss, but the memory of her smile was as clear as anything that had ever happened in his life.

Getting quickly to his feet, he joined the man on watch.

The stone ruins were unclear in the night fog. He didn't know the guard was Trang until Chan reached him. "A quiet night," said his friend as he approached. "Are you well?"

Aftereffects of the dream must have shown on his face. He opened his mouth and was about to tell Trang the strange dream and ask what it might mean, but he only made a wordless sound of anger. "Yes, of course I'm well."

It wouldn't do to let anyone know his mind was wandering far from his sworn duty. That was a good way to find oneself in a lively Communist session of self-criticism. Better to keep such a vision a secret, even if he couldn't pretend it meant nothing to him. *I guess I have at least a trace of the peasant mentality myself,* he thought ruefully.

"There!" said Trang suddenly, pointing toward the jungle.

Monkeys scattered through the treetops, heralding the quarry's approach.

Chan barked an order, trying to keep his voice low enough so that only his men heard. He watched with satisfaction as his squad hid among the walls of the ruins, rifles at the ready.

It was anticlimactic to see five children come bounding along the path. They were acting carefree for hostages, Chan thought, shouting and teasing each other as they came. He was more interested in the two who followed them: one was a young woman with long black hair. By her complexion and features she could be a European, even perhaps an American.

With a shock, Chan saw that the one with her was indescribable as far as race or country of origin. He wasn't even sure that such a creature could be human, but the children didn't seem to notice. They danced about him and pulled on his clothing, begging for attention. Chan saw that the strange one carried a string on which hung three large fish.

Chan stood watching the odd collection of people come closer, trying to reconcile his idea of CIA spies kidnapping children with this intimate scene.

Trang made a questioning sound under his breath, and Chan suddenly remembered his responsibilities. Lifting his hand he gave the signal for his men to come out of hiding. The alien creature dropped the fish he was carrying. He and the woman hid some of the children behind themselves.

"I'm Lieutenant Chan. You will come with us. If you attempt to struggle, you'll regret it."

"We were bothering no one here."

Chan was surprised to hear the alien speaking perfect Khmer. It seemed he had even picked up the local dialect, as if in echo of Chan's own words.

"That is not the point," said Chan, stepping forward to confront them. The alien looked even worse up close. "You have in your custody five of our children. Children that will be needed in the long struggle to create a new society." He was now close enough to reach down and stroke the head of the nearest child, a little girl with a tattered doll.

"Leave me alone!" she shouted, slapping at his hand and then running to grasp the leg of the alien and hide behind it. Gently Scorpio disengaged her, and the young woman picked her up.

"It seems you've had time to brainwash these poor children," said Chan, loudly enough so the troops heard. He felt he was making a poor showing as leader. "But they must come with me. Now!" As he spoke, he grabbed the wrists of two children standing near him, as if to drag them away.

"Let go of them!" shouted the alien, and he came for Chan, long arms flailing.

Chan felt only a momentary surge of fear at the creature's strangeness, and then his training came into play. Easily fending off the clumsy blows with a series of swift blocks, Chan shifted his weight to one foot and delivered a powerful side kick that sent the alien crashing into the underbrush. Now he felt that things were going much better; he was setting the proper example as a leader. He took a cat stance and awaited the alien's next charge, but suddenly he felt himself attacked from behind. He only kept himself from lashing out at the last minute, when he realized the children were grabbing at his clothing and wrists. He couldn't disengage them in time to defend against the alien's lumbering attack, and he was enveloped in a bear hug. The two of them staggered about the path, locked together, and Chan heard himself shouting, "Fire! Fire!" knowing at the same moment that his own body was in the line of fire. He heard the sharp report of a shot, but the bullet sliced harmlessly through the trees, far above their heads.

The firing had no effect on the alien. He and Chan fell to

the ground and rolled further into the jungle. Over the alien's shoulder, Chan saw that the woman had picked up a stout tree branch and only waited for an opening to use it.

He heard his men shouting and the rustling and cracking noises as they approached the foliage. It was then that everything was blotted out by a sudden flash of light and the loudest roar Chan had ever heard.

Trang and the others could do no more than dive into the brush and cover their heads as the buried mine exploded. He had a bad feeling inside as he raised his head and looked beyond the trees. Fire was snapping and burning in the dry grass and debris of the forest floor, as well as on several low-hanging vines. Otherwise there was only a crater of raw earth to mark where his friend had once been.

"It is my fault," he said quietly. "I fired over their heads instead of protecting Chan."

"You couldn't do anything else," said the man beside him.

Trang didn't want to approach the crater, but with the others in his squad there, he didn't feel he could lag behind. The children, who had been close to the explosion, had been knocked down, but he saw that now they were trying to rise to their feet. He and the others went to them and checked for wounds, but there were only a few shallow cuts on their faces.

"They were so close," said one of the men. "It must be a miracle they weren't hurt much worse. It's like something absorbed part of the explosion's force."

Trang gave the man a look to silence him. He didn't want to hear more peasant superstitions when his friend lay dead in the jungle. Unable to put off the worst any longer, Trang approached the crater. It was a shallow depression, the raw earth packed smoothly. The man had been right that there was something funny about this explosion. The strangest of all was that, though Trang had steeled himself for the sight of Chan's body, no trace of either body was found in the crater or in the small clear space around it.

"He's not here," said one of the men, and the others exchanged frightened looks.

"Search the jungle," said Trang, not even realizing he had taken over the command. "There has to be some sign of them."

The men milled around, searching the surrounding jungle. Trang saw the frightened expressions on their faces when nothing was found and the way they whispered together when he wasn't looking directly at them. New at the command, he still knew enough to realize that if he didn't order them out quickly, they would desert.

"Let's take the children and return," he said. "After all, that was our mission. We can carry it out in Chan's memory."

The children were beginning to hug each other and cry. Trang picked up the nearest, a skinny girl, and signalled that the others were to bring the rest.

When they had gone, Leah stirred in the cradle of ropy vines and foliage high in the branches of a tree and nearly fell out before she realized where she was. *The blast*—she thought, and could get no further. There had been something important about the explosion, but her mind slipped away from it.

Her vision blurred with afterimages and her ears still rang. She lay still for awhile, letting the wind rock her in her makeshift hammock. Two small monkeys crept toward her through the leafy canopy, watching her with bright, beady eyes. Slowly, she began to remember what had happened. She had been trying to get a chance to hit the soldier, when the blast—

She forced herself to get beyond it. The blast had encompassed both Scorpio and the soldier. Some freakish current must have thrown her up here. She began to struggle free of the vines wrapped around her body. Monkeys bolted, chittering in fear. After awhile, she managed to reach over to a stout tree branch and pull herelf clear of the hampering vines. Clutching the branch and scrabbling with her feet, she began to climb down.

When she reached the ground, she took a moment to move about and try to assess the damage. Though her clothing was charred and torn, her arms and legs still seemed to work. Slowly, her sight and hearing were returning to normal. *I'm all right,* she thought, *but what of Scorpio and the children?*

She saw the crater and went to study it. *If there were bodies, the other soldiers may have carried them off,* she told herself, *but there was something I should be remembering about the blast.* She sat beside the crater for some time, and at last it came to her. In the heart of the explosion she had seen an expanding golden sphere. *The orb. Did the orb protect him? And if it did, then where is he?* She looked about for the children, but only found Vanna's old doll, soot-blackened and ground into the dirt, evidently by someone's heel as he had walked past.

There weren't any answers here. She looked over toward the ruins. She knew that the tower room they had created was snug and comfortable. There was plenty of food, but suddenly the idea of staying, where they had begun to be so happy, repelled her. She considered searching for the children, but felt dizzy and confused. The explosion must have shaken her up worse than she had thought. She could only think of returning to Phnom Penh, where she at least still had two friends. Maybe they could help her somehow.

● ● ●

The trip back was a blur. She remembered sections of road, the wrinkled face of an old peasant who gave her a lift in the back of his old truck. Twice she saw troops of black-clad soldiers patrolling, but she managed to find hiding places both times. By some miracle she made it back to the city, but it seemed little like the city she had left. In place of the lively traffic were empty streets. Cars either sat where they had been abandoned by their owners, or lay in scattered and blackened heaps, the work of vandals. Where thriving businesses had stood were empty buildings and boarded-up windows. Piles of litter and rubbish were everywhere. The restaurant where she had met Roz and Ian was deserted, except for a teenager with a surly air who was mopping the floor.

"Nothing to eat here," he said to her, flapping his hands in a shooing motion. "Communist Youth Corps will soon be holding a meeting. Outsiders are not wanted."

When Leah turned toward the door, she felt as if her last hope had been extinguished.

"Leah, where have you been?" Roz and Ian rushed up to her. She had been so far and so much had happened that she didn't know how to answer.

"We thought we'd come by our old hangout one last time," said Ian.

"You don't look so good," said Roz.

"I guess I was pretty shaken up by the explosion," said Leah. "I've been dizzy and things have been blurred sometimes."

"No food here," said the teenager, as if ready to go into his spiel. With Roz supporting Leah on one side and Ian on the other, they left the restaurant and found a bench along the street where Leah could sit down. After she had told them about the explosion, she added the part about having seen the shape of the golden orb within the flame.

Roz and Ian exchanged looks. "She's talking out of her head," said Roz. "Maybe she has a concussion, and I don't think there's a chance of getting adequate medical treatment in the city now."

"What can we do?" asked Ian. "The chopper is coming for us this afternoon."

"Things have gotten dangerous here," Roz explained very slowly to Leah. "Foreign journalists have been ordered to leave. Hasn't your paper made arrangements for you?"

"I don't work for a paper," said Leah. The pretense didn't matter anymore.

"See, I told you she was an imposter," said Ian.

"Then you busted your buns to make contact with the local papers for an imposter," said Roz. "We all wanted to help those kids, and we would have, except for the invasion. What happened to the children, Leah?"

"If they weren't killed by the explosion, they were taken to a cooperative in the North," said Leah. "I have to think they're still alive. They're all I have now, especially with the two of you leaving."

"You're going with us," said Roz.

"You're nuts," said Ian. "We don't have any idea who or what she is. She probably doesn't even have a passport."

Leah shook her head.

"I'll talk fast," said Roz. "Several refugee camps have already been set up in Thailand. I'll convince the pilot to take her to one of those. She should be able to get proper medical care there."

"I can't leave without knowing what's happened to the children," said Leah.

Between the two of them, Roz and Ian convinced Leah that she had to leave long enough to get medical treatment.

She was reluctant to go, but she had to admit that she hadn't felt right since the explosion.

That afternoon Leah accompanied her friends to an open field just outside the city. She looked about, but from here she could see no vehicles, or even any road. "Are we going to walk?" she asked innocently.

"It'll be here soon," said Ian, evidently taking her words for sarcasm.

Leah heard a strange sound from the sky, different from the sounds the planes made on their bombing runs. This was a rhythmic thup-thup-thup. A moment later she was amazed to see a kind of carriage floating toward them through the air. The noise was the sound of slender blades revolving above them.

"No, we're not going to—fly," said Leah, struck suddenly with the impossibility of it.

"I hope you're not a white-knuckle flyer," laughed Roz. "We have to get out, and this is the fastest way to do it."

A whirlwind was created as the craft came straight down; debris and dust was thrown into Leah's face, her further objections lost in the noise. Roz and Ian, still supporting her, walked her to the door and boosted her up inside.

Roz leaned forward in earnest conversation with the pilot. Evidently she was pleading Leah's case. The noise made their conversation impossible to follow, but after a few minutes the man looked back at Leah and nodded curtly.

"You're in," said Ian.

Leah's eyes were squeezed shut as the craft actually started to leave the ground, but eventually she had to open them, if only out of curiosity. As she had feared, they were in the middle of the air with the ground receding rapidly. Roughly geometric patterns of roads and rice paddies became apparent as they rose higher.

"The pilot is going to leave you off at Khao I Dang. You'll

be safe there." said Roz. "Maybe after all this is over we can meet in Cambodia again."

"We're really flying," said Leah looking down on a milky skim of low-lying clouds. "Like birds! It's a miracle!"

Roz and Ian exchanged looks again. "She has definitely got a concussion," Ian said.

Chapter
6

*C*han opened his eyes. He was lying on a spongy hillock, his feet in tepid water, the fronds of a huge fern arching over his face like a green parasol. A swarm of gnat-like insects gathered about him, until his slapping motions scared them away. He sat up and looked around. A few yards away lay the alien, clutching a blackened sphere to his chest. He was moaning and tossing like a man in a bad dream.

Bit by bit the details of the explosion came back to him. It had happened so quickly he hardly had time to realize he had died.

He had died. They had struggled off the path and rolled onto a hidden mine. It had exploded and almost certainly they had both died.

Chan had had a traditional Buddhist upbringing. As a child he has been told that one was born over and over into new lives, and the status in the next life was dependent upon what one had done in the present life. But the Communist Youth Corps had given him another outlook. "Pray to Buddha and wait for him to give you something to eat," they said. And, "The Buddhist religion is the cause of our country's weakness." He had learned to put all old-fashioned notions of religion and afterlife behind him. Life was for the strong and the present moment was enough. Thus, he stood up and looked around, utterly confused as to what had happened and where he was.

What he could see of the sky beyond the burgeoning growth of unfamiliar foliage was an intense blue. He filled his lungs. There was something about the air here. There wasn't even the faintest trace of smoke or gasoline fumes, and just breathing gave him an almost transcendent feeling, as if he were breathing a slightly different mixture than his body had been used to.

He could see no familiar landmarks, only lush foliage and brackish-looking pools of water. He saw that the pools gave way to open water a little further on. Three large islands and a small one were visible through the rising fog. Far off in the sky he saw the V-shapes of soaring birds.

He knelt by one of the pools and studied his reflection. He wouldn't have been surprised if a totally new face had looked out at him, but except for a few sooty smudges on his cheeks, he was unchanged.

I'm in a new world, he thought, *but I'm the same me. Therefore even though I died, I haven't been born into a new life. But what if there are way stations between lives, where one can reflect on past deeds or gain wisdom to do better next time?*

He looked over at Scorpio, now beginning to sit up and check himself for broken bones. *What if such a one were sent as a guru, or teacher, to help the soul along the path to a new life?*

He went over to where Scorpio was sitting and knelt before him. "Are you all right, Master?" he asked, though he supposed that was a stupid question considering that they were both dead.

The alien looked at the blackened sphere in his hands and shook his head sadly. Chan wondered if it were some sort of talisman. Even if it had once worked magic, it looked as if the explosion had damaged it, charring its surface. The alien appeared distressed at its appearance.

"Can you tell me where we are, Master?" said Chan.

"I'm Scorpio, not your master," said the alien. "And no, I'm afraid I can't tell you where we are. Or even when we are, for that matter."

Chan felt properly chastened. Of course, he was not ready for the mysteries of the cosmic way station, so newly dead as he was. Still, he had the impression that their journey hadn't necessarily been any easier for Scorpio than for himself.

Scorpio gave a sigh of resignation. "I see that we're near water," he said, indicating the glitter of sun off the water's surface. "At least we won't starve." Inexplicably, the alien kicked off his shoes and began to walk toward the sea.

Chan looked at him without saying anything. He had never thought of eating in connection with the afterlife. But Scorpio was the guru. He followed, almost becoming mired with the first step. He noticed that Scorpio had slightly webbed toes, an advantage for this marshy terrain.

Chan studied the three islands as they approached the water. They were closer to the shore than he thought and barren, not even supporting a thin growth of foliage. Their pebbly gray texture looked strange to Chan; it didn't resemble earth or rock.

The bank leading down to the sea was fringed with growth—more ferns and horsetails, and thick-trunked shrubs with spiny leaves. As Scorpio and Chan stood there, a head shaped something like a horse's, but much larger, rose from the water, and with mouth open moved straight toward them. They both yelled and jumped back as the mouth with its rake-like teeth closed on a clump of ferns.

The head with its tiny, myopic eyes was still for a few moments, the huge jaws working at bringing the mass of foliage inside its mouth. It took some time for the sight and sound of the two intruders on the bank to register, then the head began to rise into the air on a neck that seemed to never end, water sluicing off the pebbly gray skin. Chan judged that it rose over twenty feet up into the air, and then the islands began to move. He watched in incredulity as he realized that the islands weren't islands at all, but unimaginably large creatures that had been lazing in the water. The head and neck they had seen was attached to the nearest one; the heads of the others were at, or a little below, water level. They blew water out of their foreheads as they raised their heads, as if their nostrils were above their eyes. Chan saw that the tiny disturbance he and Scorpio had made unsettled the beasts, for slowly they began to move away.

For all their size, they moved gracefully in the water as though their bodies were buoyant. They didn't seem afraid so much as disgruntled (Chan supposed the surprise of seeing two humanoids amid the foliage of the bank was rather like finding a bug in one's rice bowl.) Using the water to float them along, they moved off, elephantine and complacent.

"What can those be, Mas—I mean, Scorpio?" asked Chan.

"How am I supposed to know? You're the earthling, though I suppose we can't be sure we're still on earth."

Chan was becoming a little disappointed in the whole master-student relationship. He was also thinking that, incredible as it sounded, there was something familiar about the idea of those huge creatures, even if he had never expected to see so much bone and muscle and flesh walking the earth.

Without further explanation, Scorpio leaped into the water. Chan stood numbly on the bank, hoping the alien wasn't just going to swim away, leaving him in this unfamiliar environment. After a few minutes, Scorpio splashed back toward the bank and threw a double handful of shells toward Chan.

Chan took off his shirt and made a sack to carry them in as Scorpio went back for another load.

"I think these should be perfectly good as they are," said Scorpio, prying open a shell and letting the slimy gray contents slide into his mouth. "But I suppose you prefer to ruin them with fire."

"Fire," said Chan distractedly, and he began patting his trouser pockets. He still had a tin of matches. *What sort of afterlife is this,* he wondered, *where you have to bring your own matches and catch your own food?*

They climbed to higher ground where the earth was drier, and Chan dug a fire pit where he could roast the shellfish. Scorpio had already greedily gorged on his raw share before Chan had finished cooking his. The shellfish were large and succulent, even though Chan burned his fingers on the heated shells. In fact, he couldn't remember when he had had such a fine meal. He realized that he had been so focused on his idea of rising through the party ranks that he had lost interest in such basic delights as good food. He looked at Scorpio with new awe. *It seems he has lessons to teach me after all,* he thought. *If I only have eyes and ears to see and hear them.*

The sun, which looked somehow larger and clearer, was setting in a wash of crimson.

"I suppose it'll be night soon," said Scorpio. "If this place has a night. I think we should seek some sort of shelter before then. If the creatures we saw are any indication of what sort of animals live here, then we'll want protection."

"They didn't act all that aggressive," said Chan, "for all their size." He was feeling lazy now that he was fed.

"I meant that they could easily step on us," said Scorpio, "or ingest us with a clump of reeds."

"Let's seek shelter," said Chan enthusiastically.

They located a narrow cave on a rocky hillside above the sea. Chan felt that it should be good protection from whatever benign species lived in the afterlife. The big beasts they had seen earlier had given him such a sense of unending tranquility as they lazed in the water and then drifted away, half swimming, half wading, that he didn't think there could be anything to fear in this world.

Chan awoke the next morning with less sense of unreality than he had felt the day before. Even though this world was unfamiliar, he decided it was more physical than spiritual. Scorpio sat in the cave entrance, rubbing the charred surface of the orb with a strip torn from his shirt. The surface beneath was gray and lusterless, and Chan could see nothing of interest in it. Chan had the idea that, before he had fully awakened, Scorpio had been conversing with the orb, though he had stopped when Chan stirred.

Embarassed, Scorpio put the orb in the pouch he still carried on his belt. "I thought we might search the surrounding area for edible nuts or roots," said Scorpio.

"We know nothing of this place," said Chan. "How do we know that we won't die in agony from eating the plants here?"

"We don't know, of course," said Scorpio. "But if we're cautious in our tasting, we should be able to find out what's safe and what's not."

"I used to be pretty good at finding tubers," said Chan. "Maybe there's something like that here."

They looked around the hillside and found some flakes of thin rock to use as knives and digging tools. They spent the morning wandering about looking for edibles. A time or two

Chan flushed what looked like a small rodent from hiding, and beetle-like insects scuttled away when he lifted a rotten log. This added to his feeling that wherever they were, this place was too detailed to be an afterlife. And he didn't feel dead.

Later in the morning, after they had gathered a good selection of plant food, they heard a sound approaching. To Chan it was like a hundred buzz saws operating all at once. Flopping down on their bellies, they crawled in the direction of the sound.

Six or seven giant beasts approached, walking upright on their hind legs and grazing on the horsetail rushes that grew in profusion. Their skins were covered with horny tubercles forming camouflage patterns of light and shadow. High crests on their heads made them look even more imposing, and from time to time they stood as high as possible on their three-toed feet and swept the crests back and forth, as if they were testing the air for scent.

Horny bills or beaks jutted out from their faces, but their formidable array of teeth were obvious from the continual harsh grinding sound of chewing the hard rushes. The lead beast looked to be over twenty-five feet long from its bill to the tip of its tail, and those behind might have been larger still; but except for their size, there didn't seem to be anything else to fear from them. They might have been oxen chewing their cuds.

"This is certainly a peaceful place," observed Chan. "All the beasts living in harmony with each other. Maybe it really is a paradise."

They were just walking by a grove of spiky-leaved trees with trunks that looked like pineapples. Chan heard the crackling of something large displacing the foliage, and as he whirled around, he saw a grotesque shape bearing down on him.

It was a huge lizard-like creature standing upright, though not erect, on heavily muscled rear legs. A long tail, held off the ground, balanced the weight of an enormous head. Its skin was green and set with small, horny plates, darker on the back, shading to ivory on the belly. Chan stood frozen, like someone in the path of an oncoming truck. As he watched, the creature opened its four-foot jaws. Its teeth were as long as knives.

He imagined its hot breath on his face, the dagger-like teeth descending, then Scorpio grabbed Chan and pulled him to the ground. Something came down heavily beside Chan's prone body, and when he opened his eyes, he saw the foot of the monster, like the talons of an enormous eagle.

Then it had gone past, and he and Scorpio rose to watch the thing making straight for the plant-eating beasts which were already taking flight. The predator had a definite side-to-side waddle in its gait, but Chan didn't find the movement the least bit amusing.

"I hoped he'd overlook us," said Scorpio. "We're a little small to be on his menu."

As Chan's heartbeat slowly returned to normal, he began to realize what the creature was.

The Communist Youth Corps was big on educational trips, and one of these was to a museum. He had marveled at the huge structure put together out of pieces of fossilized bone, and had been even more surprised to find that it wasn't an imaginary creature, even though the size of the skeleton stretched credulity. That trip had inspired a binge of reading in dusty old books from the city library.

"That was a tyrannosaurus," said Chan. "The pictures weren't quite right, but— We're in earth's past!"

"Well, at least we're still on earth," said Scorpio.

"But that doesn't tell me how we got here," said Chan.

"Or"—he hardly dared to add this—"how we could get back."

"The orb brought us here," said Scorpio, "but I'm afraid it's not going to take us anywhere else. In protecting us, it acted on its own to jump through time, but it absorbed part of the explosion."

Chan felt a hysterical laugh building, but suppressed it. He said, straight-faced, "You mean we took a great leap backward?"

Chapter
7

*T*he Hunter roused from lethargy as he saw his orb spiking with brilliant light. After all this time, he had almost given up. He had searched the city and questioned many of the inhabitants, but they knew nothing of the Aquay and his human companion.

Lethor had been glad when the trail led here, because it was likely that Scorpio had arrived accidentally. Not only were the natives backward, they were participating in the mass insanity humans called war. Lethor understood aggression well enough, but the human methods of war were most unorganized. He had had to keep moving in and out of orb space to avoid patrols, but now that the city had been evacuated, he had dared to take up residence in an abandoned house.

If Scorpio had the least control of the orb, Lethor decided, he wouldn't have ended up here, and Lethor had begun to fear that Scorpio was gaining a measure of control. Scorpio and the human female had escaped from him far too many times already. Even though the Aquay appeared weak and harmless like all his kind, he had managed to kill Lethor's companion Ardon. Lethor hadn't recovered from that yet,

and never would. The beta had been chemically bonded to
him since birth to be his perfect servant. He had considered
returning to his homeworld to acquire another beta, but he
knew it wouldn't work out. All he could do now was to get
revenge for Ardon's death.

Once here, Scorpio's orb had become completely inactive,
and Lethor's orb couldn't trace Scorpio's unless it was being
used.

It was being used now with a vengeance, if the leaping
tongues of light inside his own sphere were any indication.
He grasped his orb and gave the command, "Follow."

When the orb bubble had expanded and burst, he was surprised by the landscape, lying wide and empty before him. If
he had thought the previous landing point had little promise,
this had absolutely none. Something moved in the distance,
and he activated his near-vision in case it was Scorpio.

He saw several gigantic beasts grazing on the tough
grasses of the swampy plain. No, gigantic didn't exactly do
them justice. They were at least twenty-five feet long. Their
heavy heads supported three horns, one of them on the nose,
and behind the head they had a protective frill of bone like a
high collar.

The Hunter had dedicated his life to the thrill of the chase,
and as he looked at these monsters, he imagined that three-
horned head with its collar of bone dominating his trophy
room. Of course, he knew he should begin to track Scorpio
and the human woman immediately, but how many times
would he have the opportunity to hunt such a magnificent
beast?

Using the orb, he brought himself closer to the animals,
who looked placid enough as they browsed on the thick foliage. When the orb began to solidify in their midst, the big
reptiles showed signs of unease, shuffling their enormous
feet and swaying back and forth.

The one closest to him, a monster with dusty gray-green skin, looked directly at the orb and its passenger now visible through the bubble's surface. It scratched the earth with its forefeet and threw back its immense head to trumpet a hoarse challenge. For all that their diet was grass and thorny foliage, the three-horned creatures were not without aggression. The orb bubble burst, dropping Lethor onto the swampy ground. He quickly picked up the orb, now grown small, and put it into its case on his belt.

Something in Lethor wanted to answer the creature's challenge, and he was checking his wrist weapon from the time the orb deposited him on the swampy ground. He saw with satisfaction that it had a fresh energy cartridge.

As his gaze fixed on the weapon, he heard a sound: the earth-shuddering gallop of the three-horn's charge. When he looked up, he saw that it had covered roughly a quarter of the distance between itself and him. He was looking at three four-foot-long horns, driven by ten tons of bone and muscle, hurtling straight toward him. It would have been easy for him to reactivate the orb, but his hunting instincts were now fully aroused and he stood his ground, lifting his wrist into position for a shot and putting the thumb of his other hand on the firing stud.

His first shot burned across the beast's back, drawing a black, charred line, but having no immediate effect on the thick hide. The second beam was deflected by the heavy bone beneath the neck frill. By this time the beast had covered two-thirds of the distance, and Lethor could see the beak-like mouth and the tiny, uncomprehending eyes. His third shot hit the huge skull dead center, but failed to immediately penetrate what must have been massive bone. He wasn't so sure that even if he burned out its brain that it would be stopped. Something that size must have its nerve tissue less centralized.

Some more civilized aspect of his personality told him this was the time to activate the orb, to escape, but his inborn hunting instincts were stronger. He sent a beam sizzling into an enormous foreleg, hoping to bring it down. Leathery skin and tough muscle blackened but resisted, and the momentum of the charge was unaffected. Now it was so close he could smell its animal odor and hear the hoarse rasping of its breath.

It was then that he realized that the beam weapon, so exact and accurate in an assassination or duel, wasn't strong enough to stop ten tons of hurtling flesh and bone with no vulnerable spots. He reached for the orb at his belt, but he judged there was not enough time, even though all he had to do was to get the device into his hand. The juggernaut was almost upon him. Desperately, he tried to leap sideways, but the hurtling weight brushed him as it passed, throwing him several feet into the dense, thorny foliage. The orb he had been trying to pick up went flying.

The three-horn's charge took it quite a distance past Lethor, but it swung about nimbly and started back. Lethor crawled about on hands and knees in the brush in search of the orb, his hard, red skin raked painfully by the thorny growth.

He never would have found the orb if it hadn't been giving off its golden glow, but he saw its gleam and got both hands on it just as the monster was on him again, lowering its head to put its formidable horns into play.

Orb light enfolded him, and he jumped as a horn thrust through the place he had just been. His arms and legs smarting from thorn cuts, Lethor toyed with the thought of returning and using the orb to help him avoid the beast's charges. It would take time, but he could eventually bring it down, even with the beam weapon. This was, of course, against the sporting code of the Hunters, but in this remote time and place, he could hardly be judged by his peers. Finally, Hunter ethics won out and he decided against it.

This is all the fault of Scorpio and his human companion, the Hunter thought. *I'll save my anger for them.*

Chan waited at the edge of the sea for Scorpio to return from another fishing expedition. A pteranodon sailed gracefully over his head, for the moment enveloping him in its shadow, and he smiled to think he had mistaken their silhouettes for those of birds the first day. If he hadn't been so distracted at the time, he would have noticed the high crest and the size. This one had at least a twenty-foot wingspan, though the creatures were literally all wings with a body no larger than that of a large barnyard fowl. It didn't flap those big wings, but flew as a glider, using its beak and crest as an automatic trim correction and the membranes between its wings and neck as elevators. Pteranodons were impossibly clumsy on the ground, but they spent most of the time in the air.

Chan had been surprised to see that pteranodons were covered in white fur. The books he had read pictured them as black and leathery, like bats; but when you thought about it, anything with that much wing area would soon trap enough sunlight to cook itself. The white fur was a perfect insulator.

I could write a book with what I've learned so far, thought Chan, but he didn't let himself get any farther with that thought, because to write the book or let anyone know what he'd learned meant he would get home. And he was relatively certain that that wasn't going to happen.

As he watched, the pteranodon circled back toward the ocean, losing altitude as it flew above the waves. With a movement that looked easy, the creature dipped its long beak into the shallows and brought out a wriggling fish. Quickly the pteranodon stored the fish in its pelican-like pouch and caught an updraft. *Now if Scorpio could just do that,* Chan thought with a smile.

Having little better to do, Chan followed its progress as well as he could from the shoreline. Finally it spiraled down toward a rocky island. *A real island,* Chan told himself, remembering his first day here.

On the island he could just make out about a dozen small white shapes. They gathered around the adult, and it seemed to be disgorging food from the pouch into the mouths of the young ones. It surprised him that pteranodons cared for their young. That didn't go along with the primitive sort of reproduction reptiles were known for, yet he felt that this creature must be different than the tyrannosaurus or diplodocus. It took a certain amount of intelligence to master flight.

"There you are," said Scorpio, approaching with two good-sized fish dangling at his belt. "I thought you were going to wait for me."

"I was doing a little nature study," Chan said, without explanation.

"Plenty of time for that, later," said Scorpio.

The rest of my life, Chan told himself, but said nothing aloud. His illusions of the alien as his own personal guru on the path to rebirth had soon been dispelled, but it was still difficult not to respect Scorpio. If he was not a celestial messenger, there was still a mystery about him. And though the orb was still dull and opaque, there was magic in it.

Chan knew because more than once he'd awakened in the night and had seen Scorpio with the orb in his hands. He held it close to his lips as if he were communing with it, and as if in answer, Chan had seen flickers of greenish light stir deep inside the sphere as if it were gathering its powers.

"Let's get the fire made. I'm starving," said Scorpio. Chan hastened to help him, only now remembering his own hunger. Even though his talisman showed signs of wakening,

Scorpio was more concerned with the day-to-day tasks of survival, as if he kept his mind on the here and now to keep himself from thinking of other times, other possibilities.

After they had eaten, and lay back in the glow of their campfire, Chan felt happier. One by one, the stars were coming out in the clear sky. In the half-dark Scorpio didn't look so alien. It was a time for confidences.

"It's peaceful here," said Scorpio.

"As long as we stay out of the way of the Tyrannosaurus rex," said Chan.

"But life isn't so bad here, is it? Sometimes I almost feel that it would be better for me to live out my life here," said Scorpio. "It would be so much simpler."

"Is that what you're looking for—simplicity and peace?"

"That's not so much to ask. On my world, peace was a way of life for my species. We never knew anything else; we took it for granted, until the Hunters arrived."

Chan was about to say that his own people had never known anything but war, but he realized that Scorpio needed to talk about whatever was troubling him, so he remained silent.

"Aggression is foreign to my nature," said Scorpio, "but when the only solution is peaceful surrender to things I know are wrong, how can I simply stand by? How can I learn to fight without aggression?" Scorpio spoke into the silence as if he spoke only to himself. Chan didn't know the alien's situation, but he felt he knew the answer to the riddle Scorpio had just posed.

"Karate," said Chan.

"Eh?" said Scorpio.

Chan stood up, and with a ceremonial bow began to perform his first *kata*, an exercise which demonstrated many of the karate techniques and stances. At the midpoint of the *kata*, he let out a loud cry of "ki," expelling air forcefully from his lungs.

When he had finished, Scorpio was looking at him intently. "Was that how you knocked me down before? You seemed to be doing some sort of dance, and then I hit the ground."

"I'm sorry if I hurt you. You were so much taller than me, I thought I needed the advantage," said Chan. "I didn't realize that—"

"I know, you didn't realize that I'm useless in a fight. I guess I just don't have it in me to be an aggressor."

"Karate is defensive only. It was introduced into China as a way for the Shaolin monks to protect themselves against marauding bandits. It is a very spiritual discipline." Chan turned his back. "Here, pretend you're going to attack me from behind."

"I'd rather not."

"Only a demonstration."

Reluctantly Scorpio rose and halfheartedly grabbed Chan. Chan thrust his arms up stiffly, breaking Scorpio's hold. In the next moment Chan's foot came down on Scorpio's instep and the alien felt the sharp point of an elbow dig into his ribs.

"I'm afraid I missed the spiritual aspects of that," said Scorpio, wondering whether to massage his foot or ribcage.

"With nothing more than the element of surprise and my own body, I can render an attacker harmless. The point of the elbow concentrates the force in a small area. I could have broken a rib, but of course I would use only enough force for my own protection."

"Defense without attack," said Scorpio. "I think I like it! But that dance you did looked complicated. Do you think I could learn?"

"I'd be glad to try and teach you," said Chan. "After all, we've little else to do here."

"What do I do first?"

"You must learn to meditate. Sit here and concentrate only on this fern frond." Chan pointed to a nearby plant.

"I want to learn to hit somebody, not study the plant life," said Scorpio.

"You must be calm and focused," said Chan. "That's the spiritual aspect I mentioned. Mind, soul and body all attuned to produce a supreme confidence."

The days fell into a routine. Between gathering plant food, fishing and karate lessons, much of Chan's time was filled, yet he was still restless. He began wandering about doing more of what he called "nature study." On one of these trips he walked along the shore, startling the tiny "antelope dinosaurs," hypsilophodon, who bounded out of his way on their long hind legs. Chan had once thought of dinosaurs as huge creatures only, but there were all kinds and sizes.

His wanderings led him along a narrow spit of land that connected to what would be an island when the water level was higher. He thought it might have some interesting animal life on it, but it proved to be barren and rocky. In a sandy depression in the ground he saw a clutch of eggs, or at least he supposed that was what they must be. They were much larger than any eggs he'd ever seen before. What really caught his eye was that these eggs were almost the exact shape of Scorpio's talisman. They were even the same golden color, mottled with black, as if they, too, had gone through an intense fire.

When he picked one up, he felt that it was warm, and he got a strange feeling. *What if this could be a talisman for me? I could ask it to take me home.*

He stood holding it in both hands for a moment, wishing, but after awhile he began to realize that the warmth had probably come from the sun. Whatever creature had laid the eggs here possibly depended upon sunlight to hatch them. It was not a talisman, after all, but it bore such an uncanny resemblance to the real orb, Chan couldn't resist taking it with him when he left. There were plenty of eggs left for whatever proud parents had left them here.

He had just begun the walk back when a flash of brilliant light almost blinded him. He cowered back, confused when he saw the shape of a humanoid inside a translucent globe. He had thought that Scorpio and he were the only humanoids in this world.

As the orb disgorged its passenger, Chan was surprised to see that the humanoid vaguely resembled Scorpio, except that he was larger, with red skin, and was either wearing strange headgear or had two curled horns growing out of the sides of his head. Chan now saw what the talisman should look like, for the orb of the stranger glowed with a golden light.

The stranger lifted his hand, as if in welcome. Chan saw that the alien wore a thick black bracelet around that wrist. Thinking that this must surely be a fellow mage of Scorpio, Chan lifted his hand in imitation and approached in a friendly way. The alien stopped fiddling with the bracelet and turned to Chan with more interest.

"Who are you?" the alien asked.

"Lieutenant Chan of the People's Army of Democratic Kampuchea," he said, realizing at the same time how ridiculous that sounded here.

"I am Lethor, the Hunter," said the alien, as if not to be outdone in the matter of titles. "I've come seeking one called Scorpio."

"I guessed that," said Chan. "You look a little like him, and you carry the same sort of talisman. Perhaps you've come to help us."

The alien's voice had a buzzing quality and his laugh was

like a hive full of maddened bees. "Yes, I've come to help Scorpio. This land is large, and empty; I would not have found you at all except for the smoke of your campfire. But what of the human woman? I have business with her as well."

"I'm afraid she was left behind when we made this, er, trip, but let's get back to camp. Scorpio will be glad to see you."

"Yes, direct me to your camp at once."

Chan was beginning to feel hope for the first time in weeks. He had seen what the talisman could do. Maybe the magician could be persuaded to send Chan back to his own time. They walked, in companionable silence, toward the camp.

Scorpio stood before the cave, practicing his *kata*. He was making good progress in mastering the movements. In fact, his lithe Aquay body gave him an edge in taking the some-times awkward positions. Still, from the elementary sparring matches he'd had with Chan, he realized that actual combat would be a lot more challenging. He was doubtful that even this philosophy could make a fighter out of an Aquay, but he was determined to persevere.

The roar of the hunting tyrannosaurus that occasionally roamed quite close to their cave made Scorpio put on a scowling expression and do his exercises with greater vigor.

After awhile, he grew weary of that and began to wonder where Chan had gone. He was often wandering about, which made Scorpio think that he was not content here. Scorpio kept trying to tell himself that it was better if he stayed in this peaceful world, even if he couldn't help seeing that the orb brightened with each passing day. It was recovering from the explosion.

The sight of it made him think of Leah. At first he had

spent hours trying to make mind contact with her, but nothing happened. Either the distance was too great or Leah wasn't receptive to his thoughts. She might even think he was dead. Though orb travel had caused a psychic link between himself and Leah, he had noticed nothing like this happening between himself and Chan. Perhaps humans differed in their sensitivity, or else he and Chan had simply not traveled together far enough. Whatever it was, Scorpio was relieved to be able to keep his thoughts to himself.

As he thought these things, he was looking idly out across the landscape just in time to see Chan and Lethor walking toward camp. Scorpio looked again to be certain. They were talking together. At first Scorpio felt betrayed. Picking up the orb in his panic, he thought of activating it to escape, even though it gave him a queasy feeling. Then he began to remember how he and Chan had worked together to stay alive in this age. He knew how crafty the Hunter was. In some way, Chan must have been tricked into showing the Hunter the location of their camp.

If he escaped, he decided Chan must go with him, though that now looked difficult. The tyrannosaurus roared again. *Hunting must have gone badly*, Scorpio thought, and in the next moment he was running down the hillside into the valley where those angry cries had come from.

It wasn't difficult to find the dinosaur. After all, when the creature threw back its head to bellow, it topped most of the trees. *Now to get his attention.* Scorpio knew that the predator would be much happier stalking its usual prey, and if any of the duck-bills were about, it would be chasing them. But the frustrated cries told him that the usual prey was not about and it might take a chance on even as odd-looking a victim as Scorpio.

Scorpio confronted the beast in a clearing. Solemnly, he made his ceremonial bow without taking his eyes off his adversary. *Respect for one's opponent*, thought Scorpio, looking up at the giant's head towering so high above him. *Yes, I think that can be arranged.* He began from a cat stance. One foot was advanced resting on the toes, in imitation of the way a cat leaves one forefoot free with which to strike. Then he advanced, throwing a series of quick lunge punches. It took the monster awhile to even focus on Scorpio—such a strange sight he must be in this innocent world—then it bellowed its hunger. The tyrannosaurus lurched forward, opening its huge jaws and moving in a waddling gait, a great deal faster than Scorpio thought possible.

The karate training allowed Scorpio to give ground and then turn quickly without losing his balance. He began to run back toward the camp. Luckily it wasn't far, because the tyrannosaur's greater stride gave it the advantage on a straightaway. To offset this advantage, Scorpio dodged about through the foliage. He estimated that he could just about stay ahead.

If all else failed, there was the orb, but he wanted to put off using it as long as possible. As he had hoped, Chan and Lethor were just reaching camp at the same time he came running up, ten tons of destruction clamoring at his heels.

Without stopping, he grabbed Chan's arm and shouted, "Run! The cave!"

They reached the entrance just ahead of the tyrannosaurus and plunged into the darkness. They cowered at the back of the cave as it thrust its skinny arm and taloned two-fingered hand in through the narrow entrance and scrabbled about for them.

"Your friend!" said Chan. "We left him outside."

"He's not a friend," said Scorpio, "and he'll be fine. He has an orb. He'll escape easily enough, but I wanted a diversion."

Outside the entrance the tyrannosaurus was bellowing and bringing down chunks of rock with its claws.

"That wasn't a bad one," Chan observed, "but another few feet and it would have been right on top of you."

Like a man contemplating his own execution, Scorpio brought forth the orb. "The friend you brought here would have gladly shot me on sight," said Scorpio.

"I'm sorry," said Chan. "He looked like you, and I thought—"

"That's all right," said Scorpio.

"With the talisman, what's to stop him from coming in here?"

"The Hunters are a desert breed. Narrow places make them claustrophobic, but I don't think we can count on him hesitating forever. The only way out is to use the orb."

"It looks as if it's recovered."

"The problem now is with me, but we must try. Hold on."

Scorpio and Chan clasped hands. Scorpio looked into Igre's endless gullet, and to him it was even more frightening than the maw of Tyrannosaurus rex.

He cast off into the darkness, but his fear only intensified. Utterly alone, he fell through time and space forever, screaming and flailing . . .

He awoke on the shore of the ancient sea. The fern fronds were shrunken, a cold wind whipped the waves into whitecaps, and the sky was opaque with dingy gray clouds. Something was falling from the sky, pattering softly on his head and shoulders. Chan opened his hand and caught several of the flakes on his palm: dry, gray ash.

"Where are we?" Chan asked. "I thought maybe we were going—"

"I'm not up to a jump that would take you home," said Scorpio, "and neither is the orb. So we jumped a few hundred thousand years down the time stream. I think we're roughly in the same place, but something has happened. It wasn't this cold before, and the sky is filled with ash."

As they watched, a group of duck-bills, grown lean and hungry looking, scoured the shoreline for the last few clumps of dying foliage.

A lone pteranodon circled overhead as if it were lost. A cold sea raged over islands that had once basked in sunlight.

"We're not going to stay here, are we?" asked Chan.

"No, I only had in mind to rest a few minutes in each place. I'll also try to move in space as well as time to confuse pursuit. The Hunter won't give up easily."

Other worlds followed, fading in and out in rapid succession. Scorpio had thought a series of small jumps would acclimate him to the use of the orb, but with each jump his fear grew.

When they came into existence on a green hillside overlooking a brilliant blue body of water, Scorpio felt like a winded swimmer crawling up onto the shore. He could go no further.

Chan looked around suspiciously for a moment, then he let out a whoop. "It is the Tonle Sap! The Great Lake! I'd know it anywhere! Scorpio, we're home!"

Chapter
8

*P*rincess Mey could hardly stand still as her maids fussed with her clothing. The skirt of a gauzy material embroidered with flowers and vines had to drape in two neat panels, with a length of cloth turned back to hang loosely over her right thigh. Then they loaded her down with ornaments; a pectoral of gold with many pendants hanging from it, several bracelets for each arm, and last, they set the ceremonial tiara on her head. It was ornamented with three flowering sprays intricately carven in gold. Each ornament was a testament to the goldsmiths' skill.

At last they had finished. A servant put her head in at the door to say that the royal palinquin awaited. This was a hammocklike affair hung on a sturdy frame, with curtains of damask all around. It was supported at each corner by a sturdy slave, each holding an ornamental handle. She allowed a servant to help her into the palinquin. With a word to the slaves, she was off through the city streets, followed by a small retinue of bearers of parasols and fans, as well as several stalwart bodyguards. These were under the direction of her chief protector, Pan, a grizzled old warrior who limped as he walked. He had been badly wounded in one of her father's campaigns, and his reward had been this position as Mey's protector. She sometimes thought he was chagrined by being given this post as caretaker of a baby princess, but over the years they had developed something of a friendship.

Mey knew she was not to look out, lest her delicate senses be offended, but she often pulled back an edge of the curtain to see the activity in the streets. Porters carried burdens on long yokes balanced over their shoulders. Peasants drove rumbling ox carts laden with produce. Peddlers cried their wares.

Her palinquin, marked with the royal seal, was given a wide berth, so they made good time, the slaves moving along at a smart trot. *I am to see the king*, Mey told herself with a delicious excitement. It almost didn't occur to her to think, *I'm going to see my father*. King Rajendravarmin II was far advanced in years. Mey, the youngest princess, seemed almost an afterthought. Though she had never lacked for riches and attention, her father was a remote figure to her. And, of course, as the *Devaraja*, he had the status of a god. One did not expect to be dandled on the knees of a god.

She was still peering out of the palinquin when they approached the complex of temple and palace that her father was having built. The last time she had been here, the place had bustled with activity: stonemasons and carpenters going here and there plying their trades, slaves and oxen sweating and grunting under the burdens of stone blocks. Though the temple was but half finished, it looked as if all activity had stopped. This gave her a feeling of foreboding. Building was one of the king's major preoccupations, and even after her father had fallen ill, he still took up residence in a completed wing of the new palace because he said it gave him energy to watch his builders at work.

She left her palinquin at the foot of a stone staircase, dec-

orated with imposing statues of Garuda, a figure that was
half-man, half-bird. Mey mounted the stairs, accompanied
by her retinue and joined by several members of her father's
personal guard.

It did not seem surprising to her that the king's personal
palace guard was made up of women, since as far as she
knew it had always been that way. These women were tall
and attractive. Only the most beautiful women were honored
by being allowed to serve in the palace. They wore short
sampots of the sort dancers wore, to give freedom of movement, and there was a certain arrogance in their bearing. Each
carried a javelin and on one arm a small round shield, covered with silver and intricately worked with the royal crest.

Mey noticed that the interior of the palace was also silent
and devoid of activity, though when she had last seen it, arti-
sans of wood and metal had been everywhere, making sure
the interior of the palace was not lacking in proper ornamentation.

She was met at the door of the audience chamber by Satha
Rau, a plump, obsequious man who had become her father's
chief advisor. His continually smiling, self-effacing manner
might charm a stranger, but Mey had always found it irritating. He wore a sampot of emerald brocade and many ornaments of gold. He carried a golden fan, the sort of gift given
by the king only to his most trusted advisors. It occurred to
Mey that a little over a year ago Satha had been only a pro-
vincial hanger-on at court.

"Ah, the little princess," he said, bowing so low his top-
knot almost brushed the floor. Mey bristled. At sixteen, she
might be the youngest of the royal progeny, but she didn't
like being called little.

"You must not stay long," he cautioned, again irritating
Mey. "Your father is gravely ill, as all in the kingdom know.

But he has a message of some importance for you, so listen well."

Mey brushed past the minister. She couldn't imagine how her father could stand the man for more than ten minutes altogether. When she entered the audience chamber, she quickly became aware that she was in a sickroom, as well. As she approached the dais where a throne had been displaced by a bed, she fell to her knees and crept forward. This turtle-like creeping was the necessary approach to a king who was also a god. Several Brahmans, or holy men, stood in attendance.

"Rise, my daughter," said a voice almost muffled by the rich hangings that surrounded the bed. It didn't even sound like her father. Quickly she approached the bed and looked into the face of a stranger. Or at least that was how it seemed, until she could make out a few familiar features in the gray, shrunken face that looked back at her. As long as she could remember, her father had been old, and for the last few years he had also been ill, but he had always retained a certain vigor.

Only by slow stages did Mey return to thinking of the man in the bed as her king, her father.

"I'm afraid I've been neglectful of you, daughter," he said as she leaned near to catch the words. "For all of your sisters I made suitable marriages. Though you are of marriageable age, for you I have done nothing. But I have been ill and consumed by my projects."

Mey felt excitement. She would not admit it, but she had become terribly worried about her unmarried state. Fourteen was the prime marriageable age, and she was sixteen. Perhaps her father had contacted a neighboring prince or high-ranking *kshatriya*, or noble, of the outlying provinces. *Perhaps I am to be married!* she thought.

"Time is so short," said the king, moving his head restlessly, as if looking for a comfortable position he couldn't quite find. "I cannot tell you all that you will need to know.

Promise me that you will rely on Satha Rau for good counsel. He has been a comfort to me."

"Of course, Father," said Mey, torn between wishing he would be more brief and concern for his pain.

"At my death, you will be crowned Queen of Kambuja Desa," said the king.

"Your pardon, Father," said Mey. "Your voice is so weak I thought you just said I was to be crowned as queen."

"I know this goes against the usual tradition, but I have no male heirs. I suppose I didn't give enough thought to it. I built mightily in stone, and so felt that I might live forever."

"You have many fine sons-in-law," said Mey.

"My daughters are all ingrates; their husbands all fools!" said the king, moving as if attempting to rise. An attendant soothed him, putting a damp cloth on his forehead. "They are not deserving. You are the last of my line, and a fine healthy girl. In time you will marry. There will be sons."

Tears blurred Mey's eyes. She felt a soft hand on her arm. "He is overtired. You must go now." She looked into the smiling, cherubic face of Satha Rau.

"Yes," she agreed, and bent down to begin the backward creeping that would take her out of the presence of the king.

Then she stood confused and weeping in the hallway, and at last was joined by Satha. "My father told me that I should come to you for counsel," she said, forgetting that she had thought of Satha as an impossible toady only minutes before. "Is he ill and out of his senses? He told me I was to be queen."

"He spoke the truth," said Satha. "Over the past few months he has quarrelled with his other daughters and their husbands. No doubt the kind of family squabbling that could be put right in time, but there isn't any time."

"But to choose me—"

"On the contrary, my dear, I thought it an excellent choice

and have recommended it to all the other ministers. It's true that no queen has ruled Kambuja within my memory, but the lineage of women has been important in the succession. And don't forget the legend of Willowleaf."

Mey knew that Kambuja's founding was based on the marriage between the Indian adventurer Kaundinya and Willowleaf, queen of the dragon folk. Willowleaf had even shown aggression at first, launching her war canoe to pillage the foreign merchantman. With a magic bow, Kaundinya pierced the canoe and subdued the warrior maiden.

"But that's only an old legend," said Mey. "How can I rule? I'm not ready!"

"Depend upon me," said Satha, moving close and patting her shoulder. "As I have supported the king in his declining years, so shall I aid you. Everything will go well. I promise it."

Mey returned to her palinquin, flustered and upset. This must have been obvious, because stoic Pan, who seldom spoke to her where others could see, came over to her. Quietly she explained to him what had transpired in the audience chamber. His calm demeanor helped her to keep from bursting into tears. "I don't understand it," she finished. "This can't be happening to me!"

"I admit it sounds strange," said Pan, "but I don't think he made such a bad choice. As you've grown, you've begun to show the beginnings of wisdom. And besides, if the king says it, it must be so."

Mey swayed along in the palinquin, thoughts racing through her mind. *If the king says it, it must be so*, she told herself. All of her worries about marriage had been put aside by this latest problem. She had been a foolish girl, she remembered. She had even coerced several trusted servants to convey her to the unfinished temple complex after dark. It was said that a young woman who danced in the temple courtyard at midnight would dream about her future husband.

She would never forget that night. She had danced in the wet grass until she was exhausted. Luckily no priests or guards had been about. She had had the eerie feeling of being watched, but she supposed that was only her guilt at using a holy place for something so mundane. Or maybe it was just the intimidating presence of the towering walls with their half-finished sculptures.

When she had fallen asleep that night, her soul had wandered through a desolation. The great works of her father had fallen into ruin, wrapped by roots like insidious snakes or half-hidden by burgeoning treetops. She didn't like to recall that dream. It was a bad omen concerning any possible marriage or family to come.

Now all her usual worries seemed like nothing at all in the face of this new calamity. Pan, who was a friend, had probably exaggerated her good points, but she wasn't a total fool. Kingship meant statecraft: dealing with fractious ministers and *kshatriya* who hoped to extend their influence. More importantly, kingship meant war. Kambuja was always at war or planning a war or negotiating a peace treaty.

Pan looked very surprised the next day when Mey told him that instead of her usual dancing practice, she wanted him to instruct her in the use of the bow.

"Are you sure, my queen?" he asked. She noted his promotion of her from princess to queen, even though she had not gone through the formalities. "You may soil your fine garments in such exercise."

"I'm sure," she said. "Bring me a weapon without delay. If the queen says it, it must be so."

Satha Rau was still smiling fatuously even after Princess Mey had departed. He hadn't even realized it for several minutes. He grimaced with disgust, frightening a passing slave. *I've had that smile pasted on my face so long it's almost permanent,* he thought. *For months I've smiled and crawled on my belly and ingratiated myself. Me—a* kshatriya *of the noble Satha family. But it's been worth it. Everything is coming together now.*

From his first moments at court, Satha had realized that a noble from the provinces, with a fine old family and holdings that rivaled those of the king's, would do best to keep a low profile. Those who attempted to overshadow the king soon lost favor. He had even heard of powerful and popular nobles meeting with "unfortunate accidents."

So he had downplayed his own power and had become everyone's friend, like a foolish old uncle that everyone tolerated and overlooked. The king had come to depend upon him, and in his illness, messages had gone out to family members, causing dissent. No one knew that Satha had engineered these small feuds, cutting the king off from his family.

Suggesting that Mey be crowned queen was a stroke of genius. He had originally thought to make a marriage between Mey and his son Feng, but although the boy was good to look at and cut a handsome figure in a war chariot, one conversation between Rajendravarmin and Feng would have sent a father's hopes crashing. For all the tutors Satha had hired, Feng remained incredibly dense. If the conversation went any further than what he fed his horses, the lad was at a total loss.

Yes, this idea to have Mey crowned queen was a stroke of genius. Rajendravarmin would be dead and out of the way, and a mere girl's head would easily be turned by the handsome Feng. With two such untried young people as Feng and Mey on the throne, they would have great need of Satha's counsel; and he would give it, in good measure. By the time Satha had returned to the king's bedside, a benevolent yet mysterious smile lingered on his lips.

Chapter
9

When they had landed, Scorpio was glad to fall onto the grass and rest with his hands over his eyes. Chan was eager to return to his troop. He wasn't sure what he'd tell them, but it was probably a good idea not to say too much. Maybe sometime he'd get around to writing that book about dinosaurs, but his work in creating Democratic Kampuchea came first. He wondered how they were doing. He'd look up Trang and find out. He was really looking forward to seeing Trang and the others. He hadn't realized what it would be like to live in a world without other human beings. Scorpio had treated him well, but his attitudes were so alien. Even though Chan had been teaching Scorpio all he knew about karate, and the alien could do all the drills, he wasn't sure it would come to anything. He wasn't doing well in the sparring. The creature might be naturally too diffident, even for a martial art.

Though he was eager to rush off and find his friends and take up his life were he had left it off, Chan was reluctant to simply abandon Scorpio here.

"I'll reconnoiter," Chan told him, "and try to find lodgings for us for the night. The peasants hereabouts might be hospitable, especially with my rank in the People's Army."

Scorpio made a noise which might have been assent; otherwise, he lay still. Chan wondered that the being could travel through time at all, as hard as it was for him. He set out across the countryside. He found that the jungle growth was more extensive here than he had remembered it, but he soon came upon a peasant's cottage, built on stilts to withstand the flooding of the Mekong in the rainy season.

He knew that peasants were happy with the old ways and loath to change, but the hut looked awfully primitive to him. Several naked children played in the dirt under the pilings, chasing the ducks and chickens and one of the Cambodian potbellied pigs. They pointed at him in a rude way as he approached, as if he were some apparition and not a fellow countryman. The farmer himself was just returning, leading his ox which was still harnessed to pull the plow.

As Chan came closer, the whole family ran out to inspect him, and now he was even more certain that something was wrong. The farmer wore only a sampot, the simple garment made of a strip of cloth wound around his loins and knotted in back, and the wife only a skirt draped about her hips.

Not even in the remotest village do people still dress like this, thought Chan.

The farm family was a bit shy. He saw them inspecting his garments surreptitiously. Still, they were friendly enough when they realized that he was of their race, and invited him to eat with them in the old-fashioned way of hospitality. Their dialect was strange, too, he noticed. There wasn't much doubt that he had not come home—not quite.

"I have a companion who is ill," said Chan. "I'd like to go and get him. A hot meal would do him good. But the illness has made him look, er, rather strange."

The family assured him that they would be glad to entertain his friend as well. The women began to stoke up the small clay baking ovens in preparation for cooking. Chan realized that ovens just like them were still in use in his own time. *Things don't change too rapidly,* he told himself. *Until he got close enough to see detail, I thought I was in my own time. I wonder if we were naive to think we could make Cambodia take the great leap forward into the twentieth century.*

Thus prepared, the primitives didn't seem too startled at Scorpio's appearance. They had a pleasant enough meal, and Chan listened eagerly to the gossip passed along by the farmer.

"They said the queen was crowned in the Great City today. All very exciting with elephants and carriages and a thousand gaudy parasols."

"I guess what they said was true," said the farm wife. "I could hardly believe they would break so with tradition and let a mere girl ascend the throne."

Chan's interest was piqued for a moment as he remembered a dream he had once had. That had been a long time ago, he thought, and after all, it was only a dream. The conversation soon turned to other topics: how fishing was in the Great Lake, and the family across the way who had bought a new buffalo.

As a culmination of the family's hospitality, they allowed Chan and Scorpio to sleep beneath the house for a night.

"Perhaps you'd like to see the Great City they spoke of," said Scorpio later, after the family had retired for the night. "It's the same one whose ruins we camped in, isn't it?"

"It would be interesting," said Chan, "but to be honest, I find myself eager to get home. It should be an easy matter for you to activate the talisman. Only a small leap to take us home."

"I-I don't think the orb is strong enough."

"It's not the orb—I've seen it glowing like a full moon.

It's you," said Chan, finally running out of patience. "What's the use of a powerful talisman when its owner hasn't the courage to use it?"

Scorpio didn't reply. He only repaired to the other side of the straw-covered space beneath the house. There was a disturbance in the straw as the alien lay down, and a potbellied pig ran out, squealing in frustration at being disturbed.

Chan lay down, too, but he couldn't sleep. He kept thinking of what he had just said. They had just come through centuries of time as quickly as blinking an eye. What if using the orb were as easy? Here he was, stuck in a backwater of history. He contemplated his life here, not all that different than the life he had already rejected once. Was he to end up grubbing in a rice paddy, when he could change worlds with the talisman in his hands?

No! came the thought, though luckily Chan hadn't spoken it aloud. Scorpio slept on. It was difficult to be silent while crawling through dirty straw that rustled under his hands and knees. Dust rose and clogged his nostrils, making him afraid that he would sneeze as he crouched over the sleeping alien. Carefully he untied the pouch from Scorpio's belt. It was only then that he remembered the golden egg he'd found. He had taken it as a sort of souvenir, and it still rested under his shirt.

With all that's happened, it's probably in a thousand pieces, he thought, but when he looked, it was all in one piece, the leathery shell having saved it from damage. It looked just as it did when he had taken it out of the warm sand. *This will fool him for awhile,* he thought, putting the egg into the pouch and refastening it. *Until I'm far away and learning the secrets of the real orb.*

Chan felt a twinge of guilt as he sneaked away from the peasants' hut, as if he were abandoning Scorpio. Still, it wasn't as if the alien had politely asked if he'd like to go time jumping. And the orb really should belong to someone with the ambition to use it.

Scorpio awoke with a feeling of unease. Work evidently began early for the peasants, for he could hear the sounds of people stirring in the house above. "Chan," he said, "I've been thinking, and it's selfish of me to keep you away from your own time. I'm ready to try to—" By this time he had realized that Chan wasn't there. A quick search of the farmyard, as he called his friend's name, convinced him that he was now alone.

Perhaps he decided to explore this world a little further, Scorpio thought. *Or even to make a place for himself here. I guess that's the only choice I gave him.*

Scorpio left before any of the peasants had come out of their house. The orb was a warm weight against his side, more of a weight than he had remembered. He hadn't walked too far before the orb pouch began to wriggle about.

"What's this?" he said aloud in his surprise, stopping to open the pouch and examine the orb. "Why, it's coming apart!" Startled, he dropped it and knelt to study the zigzag lines crossing its surface. The orb was really moving now, hopping vigorously in the dirt of the road as Scorpio looked on. After a moment, a long yellow beak made its appearance, followed by a tiny black eye.

I've been tricked, thought Scorpio as the egg made violent movements and was torn apart by a struggling white body. The pteranodon chick stretched its cramped wings and blinked its black eyes. After a moment it was able to hop across the ground using its wing joints to propel itself forward while the wings themselves stuck out at awkward angles. Scorpio remembered the big flying creatures and was amazed at how small the chick was. It fit easily in his cupped hands and was light and downy as a ball of fluff.

"Chan shouldn't have played this trick on both of us," said Scorpio. "You'll probably find this world strange, little one, but you'll have to try and make your way here, even as I have to." He remembered that the pteranodons were fish catchers. With the Great Lake nearby, this one might even survive.

This is what he told himself as he put the little creature down and began to walk away. He had only taken a few steps when he heard a plaintive honking sound, much louder than it should have been from so small a being. When he looked back, he saw that the baby pteranodon was following him with vigorous hops.

"No, no, little one. I'm not your *Ta*. Go along now." He made a shooing motion, hoping to scare it into the bushes at the side of the road, but it kept coming, covering a lot of ground for one so small. It only stopped when it reached Scorpio's feet, where it jumped up and down, opening its long beak hungrily.

Though he didn't want the responsibility, he could see by now that the chick needed at least some sort of parental care. He picked it up and cradled it in the crook of his arm.

Two weeks later, Scorpio toiled up the path to the camp he had set up on the shore of the Tonle Sap. He told himself he wouldn't have taken on this responsibility if he had realized how much fish a young pteranodon required. As he chopped his catch into bite-sized pieces, the pteranodon hopped around him, giving its peculiar honking cry. It now had a wingspan of about three feet. *I wonder when they learn to fly*, thought Scorpio, with visions of a happy pteranodon soaring into the sunset and himself liberated from fatherly chores.

After it had fed, he lifted it up and was again surprised at its hollow-boned lightness. "Your body weighs nothing at

all," he told it. "You're all wings. Wings, yes, that's a name
for you," he added, not really sure why the creature needed a
name at all, since they would be parting ways. *And soon I
hope,* he thought. *I must find Chan and return him to his own
time. And Leah, I wonder if she's forgotten me by now. I wonder if she's taking care of the children.*

The next day Scorpio was fishing as usual and was just
bringing his catch to the shore, when he heard a honking cry.
He looked up and saw Wings teetering on the edge of the
bank, stretching out its wings but going nowhere.

He couldn't help laughing at the sight of the desperate little creature honking and hooting at the edge of the precipice,
wanting to get to Scorpio yet not knowing how. "Fly, fly!"
shouted Scorpio, spreading his arms and running along the
lake's edge. But after a moment he realized his pantomime
was doing no good, so he ran up the path, and taking the
pteranodon in both hands, pushed it gently toward the edge.
"With none of your kind about you've forgotten your
wings," said Scorpio as he nudged his foundling over the
bank. For a moment he held his breath, afraid that Wings
might plummet straight down, pinions furled uselessly.

In the next moment he caught his breath as the young pteranodon extended its wings, catching an updraft and riding up
effortlessly into the blue sky. Once aloft, Wings didn't want
to return to earth. He swooped, circled, and slid down toward the surface of the lake. A quick movement and he
brought a fish neatly out of the shallows and deposited it in
his throat pouch.

"Then it is goodbye," Scorpio said into the distance. He
couldn't help feeling a pang of regret, even though this
meant he was now free to follow his own path. The white
wings had dwindled against the sky as the pteranodon
sought deeper water, perhaps better fishing.

Scorpio gathered his gear, what little there was, and set

out to find the road to the Great City. He was trudging along a few hours later, feeling somewhat sorry for himself, when he passed a thin figure dressed in ragged clothing.

"What are you staring at?" asked the man.

"I'm sorry to see you in so bad a state," said Scorpio.

"I could say the same about you," said the man.

"I mean so thin and ragged. Can I help you in any way?"

"I care nothing for the world's goods," said the man. "I'm on a pilgrimmage to the temple of Wat Phu to do homage to Krishna. I—" The man was looking upward with a fixed expression. "The air dragon!" he exclaimed.

Scorpio looked up and saw Wings banking against the wind.

"Evil days are upon us," shouted the man, and took to his heels.

Scorpio calmly waited for the pteranodon to land and come hopping up to him. He patted the tall head crest. "You're not really ready to leave the nest yet," he said, "and maybe I wasn't ready to let you go. Anyway, you can see what sort of welcome we'll get from the natives."

Mey sighted down the shaft, the wind from the speeding chariot blowing her hair out of the careful shape her maids had created that morning. The target was approaching too quickly. Determinedly she drew back on the bow and sent the arrow winging.

"A hit!" she shouted.

Pan grinned back at her over his shoulder, most of his attention on keeping the horses under control. He wore his old fighting garb: a sampot and short jacket. She decided he was enjoying her military education as much as she was. As they turned and came back past the target, Mey saw her arrow caught in the very edge of it.

"Well, it's not dead center," she admitted, "but I am improving."

"It's much better than the first day when you shot the floor of the chariot. I feared for my one good foot."

Mey hugged the old soldier impulsively. "When I was told I was to be queen, I was all aquiver like a foolish girl meeting her betrothed. You gave me the confidence to try and live up to my royal heritage."

She remembered her sadness upon hearing that the king, her father, had died, but she had been brave enough to follow her father's last instructions and let herself be crowned queen. Then, at the coronation procession there was so much excitement, so much smiling and cheering, she had begun to smile herself and to wave the heavy golden sword about like a conquering hero. *If they think I'm queen, maybe I am,* she told herself. She had determined then to grow into her duties as queen.

"Who can worry about a marriage when there's an entire kingdom to administrate? So many duties—"

"You are not thinking of marriage, then?" asked Pan.

"No, at least not now. Why should you think so?"

"No reason—well, I shouldn't repeat palace gossip."

"You should repeat it to me!" she said, startling herself with the commanding tone of her voice.

"The gossip is that you are interested in young Feng, the son of Satha Rau."

Mey laughed. "Old Satha was sure to bring his son to my attention. 'A handsome boy, don't you think? A graceful rider.' All the while smiling that obsequious smile that makes his face look like it's about to crack in two."

"It's quite true that Feng is an expert horseman and, I suppose, good to look at—if one is a woman, that is."

"Pan, I suppose you've never talked to him. Tried to talk is more like it. I asked how he liked the ballet of the Ramayana, which was performed in the palace that evening. He stammered and said he had gotten confused with all the people 'running around' and then he had fallen asleep. Can you imagine not appreciating the beauty of the dance? He's stupid enough to go hunting for crocodiles using his fingers as bait."

"The word in the palace is that Satha has returned to his lands to begin gathering the goods and livestock that will be offered for your hand."

"If he does, he's premature in planning the nuptials. Nothing happens around here without the queen's decree."

"As you command," said Pan. "Shall we try it again?"

Mey nocked a new arrow and sighted down the shaft. "I shall imagine Satha's smile in the center of the target," she said sweetly.

Pan laughed as they swept by the target, and the queen's arrow hit dead center.

Chapter 10

*C*han trudged, footsore and weary, along the road leading to the Great City. For a long time he'd lived in a cave, like a crazed hermit, convincing himself that using the talisman was a matter of proper meditation. The orb had only lain there, radiating its golden light as he took one position after the other, bending his body pretzel-like until one day he'd simply come blinking into the sunlight and realized that figuring out how to use the orb was probably beyond him.

Things went a little better after that. Since he knew he couldn't get the orb to take him home or to do anything at all wondrous, he was able to use it to astound the locals. So far it had been good for three chickens, a basket of rice, and passage on a sailing ship cross the Tonle Sap.

Now he was approaching the Great City. Traffic on the road increased: lumbering carts fastened together with rattan and drawn by hump-backed cattle, fine carriages with trappings of brass with small horses or long-legged racing oxen in the traces. And plenty of foot traffic: beggars and holy men, peddlers and rogues.

Remembering what it was like to walk in the ruins of the

Great City, he had a strange feeling as he saw it very much alive: merchants selling their wares in open stalls, porters carrying burdens, wealthy citizens in palinquins. He felt as if he walked amid ghosts, for all that they looked solid and the noises and smells of the street impinged upon his consciousness: cries of peddlers, scents of ripe or rotting fruit, dung in the streets, the groan and rumble of wheels over paving stones.

I'm glad I got to see this, he thought, *even if it means I can't go home.* He sighed, realizing that if he wanted to eat, he'd better go into his act.

"I am Chan the sorcerer," he cried. "I carry the moon under my jacket. Pay me and you shall see it!"

"Do you think we're stupid countryfolk?" said a sweating porter, pausing to rest in the shade cast by the overhang of a roof. "The moon under your coat. Well, I have a goat under mine; hear it bleat?" He made rude baaing sounds until the crowd was laughing raucously.

"No doubt it smells as if you have a goat under there," said Chan calmly, "but I'm willing to let you have the first peek, for nothing. Then you can tell the others of the miracle."

"See what a great wit he is," said the porter. "Well, let him laugh it off when I expose his tricks." The man lumbered forward as Chan opened his jacket just enough to show the orb, radiating its golden light.

The porter jumped back. "It glows!" he shouted. "I think it must be a great evil! Surely it is nothing natural." Muttering what must have been a warding spell, the porter slouched away.

It didn't matter. His reaction was an excellent come-on. The curious lined up, dropping whatever they had to barter at Chan's feet.

After Chan had eaten, he wandered by the temple complex to watch the work in progress. Slaves were hauling on ropes, trying to get a large, awkward statue of a five-headed horse to the top of a pedestal.

"I see the construction continues," he said idly to a guard standing in front of a stone staircase.

"King or queen, the building goes on," said the man.

"I'd like to see her," said Chan, "your queen."

"It's unlikely a street rogue like yourself will ever get an audience with the queen," said the guard in an amused way, as if he were enjoying the idea of a ragged idler like Chan paying court to the queen herself.

"Never mind," said Chan. "I'm sure I'd be disappointed." Nothing could compare with the woman in his dream. Too bad she wasn't real.

Several days later Chan had run out of food. *Time for the moon to rise,* he told himself. *The traffic flows well before the temple complex. Let's have a try there.*

No sooner had he lined up a number of prospects than he heard an angry voice and found himself surrounded by burly men carrying javelins.

"This is a disgrace," said the man who appeared to be in command. "Practically on the temple grounds."

"Stand away or be burned by the golden light!" Chan shouted suddenly, and pulling the orb from his coat, brandished it about.

Several soldiers hit the ground as if they were being fired upon by arrows. Two more took to their heels. In the confusion, Chan began to run. He skidded around a lion statue and headed back for the street where he hoped to lose himself in the traffic.

He thought he was going to make it until he heard someone cry, "Halt," and a well-thrown javelin hissed past his head. Passersby on the street scattered, leaving Chan an easy target. He stopped in answer to the command, but wasn't sure whether it was soon enough to keep the eager soldiers from throwing their entire armory at him.

The commander approached him nervously, eyeing the orb in his hand, but when Chan made no further threatening gestures with it, he became more confident. Chan heard one soldier whisper to another, "Should we confiscate this strange device?" But no one did. He was marched back toward the palace at javelin-point.

Mey sat on the throne decorated with lotus blossoms and the heads of fierce *nagas*. Her small feet, whose soles had been dyed a stylish red, didn't quite reach the floor, but everyone pretended not to notice. As sovereign, part of her duty was to give audiences to people with requests, to settle the more important legal matters of the kingdom, and to sit in judgement on high-ranking criminals. There were minor functionaries to handle routine matters, so Mey's duties in this regard were always fairly light. At first she had felt uneasy in the audience room, as if someone would jump up and shout, "She can't judge you. She's but an untried girl and knows nothing!" But no one did, and little by little she became more comfortable with the idea: the sovereign can do no wrong, whoever the sovereign happens to be at the moment. *A lucky philosophy for me,* she thought.

Today a minor functionary leaned toward her and whispered the details of the next case. It was a relief not to have to look into Satha's face, although she was uneasy about what he was doing at his country home. It didn't quite occur to her to fear him—not good old jovial Satha.

"But this sounds like a common street crime, a rascal that preys on the stupidity of the common folk. I'm sure there are many such, but it is hardly the business of a queen!"

"Begging Your Majesty's pardon," said the official, bending low as if trying to avoid the queen's wrath. "It's true that there are many would-be sorcerers plying their trade, but there is the barest possibility that this man *is* a sorcerer."

"You said he's been in custody for several days," said Mey. "Doesn't it occur to you that a real sorcerer would have burst out of any prison?"

"Indeed it seems likely, Your Majesty, but the reports said that he has a magical device of some sort, and the guardsmen feared to take it from him else its magics might taint them."

"Superstitious fools. Well, bring him in. Let's get it over with."

The official crouched down and crawled backward from her presence. When the guard came in they, too, took their positions of humility, not realizing at first that their prisoner had not bowed but was standing bolt upright among them. Worse, he was staring straight at the queen, not in an impertinent way, but as if someone had taken a hammer and hit him between the eyes.

A guard noticed and pulled the prisoner by the wrist, hissing at him, "Fool, don't you realize the proper obeisance before the queen? Bow down!"

There was a flurry of outrage among the ministers and officials in attendance, but the prisoner continued to stand and stare. A zealous guard rose partially to his feet and poked the prisoner sharply with his javelin.

"Kill him," shouted one of the ministers, and the guard looked around in confusion, then tightened his grip on the spear.

"Enough," said Mey, raising her hand. The guard froze. "Stranger, do you realize you could lose your life because you refuse to stop staring?"

"I can't help it," he said. "I didn't think I'd ever see you again. I didn't think you even existed. So if they have to kill me, I guess it's all right."

"I fear the man is demented in some way. It would be

wasteful to spill his blood," said Mey to her ministers, but secretly she was pleased by the stranger's face and his single-mindedness, especially when it focused in some way on her. One could not grow up as a princess and be totally devoid of vanity. "Bring him nearer and I'll hear his case." Behind her the ministers muttered, unhappy with this new precedent, though of course there was nothing they could do once she had spoken.

"I'm sorry if I stared," said Chan. "This will sound strange, but I fell in love with you in another world, another time." He was now beginning to recover from whatever trance he had been in. He began to look more intelligent, and more frightened.

"It does not sound strange at all," said Mey. "Everyone knows we pass through many incarnations on the Wheel of Rebirth. We could have been beetles under the same log."

"That sounds wonderful."

"Let me see the fabulous magical device you're said to own," said Mey, becoming businesslike to cover a sudden embarrassment. He had made beetles under a log sound like something intimate, rather than something disgusting. Quickly he produced a round object from beneath his jacket. Mey caught her breath at its beauty. She had lived with beautiful artifacts all her life, the best products of the goldsmiths' art. This was something apart. It glowed with steady light, and when she dared to reach out and put her hand on it, she felt a tingling in her palm and then a great feeling of well-being washed over her. She knew in that moment that the orb had magic in it, whether or not this man was a sorcerer.

"Do you like it? It's yours," Chan said eagerly, apparently delighted that it had captured her attention, like some bauble a lover gives a betrothed. She shied away from that thought and the gift. Gently she handed it back to him and cautioned him to hide it again.

"It's but a worthless trifle," she told the ministers, "and he's a harmless madman."

"Let me dispose of him for you," said an officious minister.

"No, the sovereign must make a show of charity as an example to the people. Find quarters for him in the palace. There must be some menial job he can do to earn his living."

Before the guards could take Chan away, there was a disturbance outside. A servant entered, crept forward, and whispered to Mey, "It's the minister Satha, Your Majesty, and his son Feng."

"Well, his place is here, among my other officials. Why does he linger outside, asking my permission to enter?"

"His visit is not as chief minister, Your Majesty, but as official business of another sort. If you'd but look out the window, you'd see the bounty: cattle, goats, horses, carriages, palinquins—all of the finest quality. Satha has come as a father to make a marriage between you and Feng, and he has brought the usual wedding gifts."

Mey knew that it was usual for the father of the bride to offer up livestock and other gifts to the groom's family, but obviously because she was a queen, the tables had been turned.

"I wish he had not done this," she told the servant. "I have no wish to humiliate him or his son publicly, but I guess there's no answer for that now. He's at the door, so bid him come in."

Satha and Feng entered, dressed in their most costly garments, amid a retinue of servants carrying parasols and fly whisks. Satha followed protocol and crouched down to approach the queen. When she gave him leave to speak, he began to declaim the usual flowery utterances that accompanied the formal making of a marriage between two wealthy folk. This was ended by a listing of all the goods that were offered as gifts.

"Only fifty goats?" said Mey, hoping a show of greed might put a stop to this.

"Make it a hundred," said Satha. "You may have as many goats as you desire."

"The truth is I desire no goats at all," said Mey, "or any of the gifts you offer. I wish you had asked me this privately, but I do not wish to marry your son."

There was a subdued whispering among the ministers and onlookers, for this was a public humiliation. They seemed to hold their breath for Satha's reaction. Then he smiled. But all the strain of holding that mock jovial expression for so many years showed in his face, making his expression terrible to behold.

"I'm sorry, but you must take your gifts and go," said Mey.

"Something you might wish to know before you act hastily, Your Majesty." Satha's words were tipped with venom. "My holdings are extensive, as you know, and to protect them, I have had need to keep a large army. I have been building it up for a number of years, and considering how things have deteriorated here during Rajendravarmin's illness, I really believe my army is larger than the troops you maintain to guard the city. Perhaps we shall have an opportunity to compare armies, because mine should be here in a few days."

Mey felt a chill. If she had just figuratively slapped Satha's face, he had given her a strong blow in return. She believed him when he said he had amassed an army. It had always seemed to her that there had to be something hidden behind that false face.

Mey felt like bursting into tears or scrambling down from the throne and running to her own private chambers. Instead she straightened herself and gave Satha a withering look. "A clash of armies is all very well with me," she said. "I shall have my attendants prepare my war chariot, and I will lead the royal armies myself. Until then, Chief Minister Satha, get out of my sight. And take your whelp with you."

Satha finally let his features settle into a fierce grimace, then without a word, he crouched down and backed out of her presence.

It's really difficult to make a dramatic exit that way, thought Mey, laughing to herself.

After Satha and son had left, and the guards and ministers and hangers-on had cleared the room, Mey walked about distractedly. She was surprised to see Pan enter the room. He was never comfortable at court and spent little time in the palace, even though as the queen's confidant he enjoyed a new status.

"Did you hear—?"

"I heard," said Pan.

"Is this situation as disastrous as it feels?" she asked with a slight smile, hoping for reassurance.

"It's that bad and worse," said Pan. "Perhaps I should have seen this coming, but I was so carried away by my memories of battle and glory I couldn't see the consequences of our games. They were only games, didn't you know that?"

"But I tried to hard to learn, and I was getting better."

"It's not your fault. Rajendravarmin let his armies grow weak as he put his resources into the building of the Great City and the temple. And though men might cheer you in the street, riding the royal elephant and waving a sword, many of them will desert at the prospect of risking death behind a girl playing at war."

"But I have given the challenge. If the queen says it, it must be right!"

"Yes, you do have the power to send thousands to their deaths and to see the city your father worked so hard to build conquered and overrun. Or you have the power to save them. Contact Satha. Plead that you were ill, not yourself, when you refused his gifts. Say that you will marry Feng."

"No! I don't love Feng."

"What has that to do with anything?"

She couldn't answer. As a young girl she had contemplated marriage as an arrangement made by one's parents. She had had little contact with young men, and so there was little opportunity to realize that one might have a particular interest in one. She hadn't thought about having that particular interest until . . . scant hours ago, when she had met the young sorcerer.

"Tell me that you'll think seriously about what I've told you," said Pan. "I'm sorry that I may have put false ideas into your head, but I wasn't lying when I said I saw in you the potential for wisdom. Think on it, and I know you'll see my point."

Later that evening, Chan was lying in the small, dank room they had given him after he had exhausted himself from cleaning the royal stables. *Somehow I pictured the outcome of our meeting as different than this,* he thought.

The door rumbled open and a servant thrust his head in. "You are called to the queen's private chambers immediately."

"But I'm tired," Chan complained, "and I'm not even clean."

"It's not you she wishes to see so much as your magic charm," said the servant. "And it's not a good idea to keep her waiting."

Mey's private apartments in the palace were as exquisite as Chan might have imagined, but the queen was more exquisite herself in a wrap of white silk with a spray of white blossoms in her hair. Several handmaidens were in the room, and they giggled as he entered. *Fine,* he thought. *I smell like a barn and she has all her schoolgirl friends in attendance.*

Mey held out her hands. "I had difficulty sleeping and I thought—"

Chan almost grasped her hands, but held back a moment.

"I thought of your wonderful orb and how it calmed my fears."

"Yes, the wonderful orb," said Chan, handing it to her and watching as she lay her hands on it and then her cheek. She sighed deeply and handed it back. Their hands touched accidentally, and they looked into each other's eyes.

"I know there's magic in this device," said Mey. "I can feel it. But you're the sorcerer. What can it really do?"

Chan was about to go into his street sorcerer routine, when he realized that at this moment the truth was more important. "I've seen it do miraculous things," said Chan, "but unfortunately not for me. I stole the talisman from a sorcerer friend—well, I was angry at him, but he was a friend. He took me journeying to new worlds and times."

Mey listened wide-eyed.

"I saw the way you sent that fat windbag packing," said Chan. "He just about popped his eyeballs when you told him you'd meet him on the field of battle. I loved it!"

Mey looked down. "I did it out of pride," she said, "to save face. His armies are no doubt more powerful than those of the City. A friend counseled me to take my hasty words back, to apologize to Satha and tell him I'll marry his son. Now that I've had time to think about things, I'm afraid that's the wisest course of all. Statecraft is as important as war, especially when the enemy has a more powerful army."

"Marry Feng!" said Chan. "You can't do that." He had drawn closer, and now Mey looked up at him in a way that made him feel that he'd take on Satha's army himself if she asked it. "Listen, the sorcerer I spoke of must still be here. He'll be angry, but I'll beg if I have to. I'll bring him here, and he'll think of a way to use the orb to solve your problem. He has to!"

"I find the idea of marrying Feng to be repugnant, too," said Mey. "After all, there are other men more worthy."

"I'll leave at once," said Chan, forgetting his exhaustion.

"A horse will be waiting for you at the Chariot Gate."

He dared a quick goodbye kiss, and the handmaidens giggled.

Chapter
11

Leah was just coming out of a patient's room with a tray when another volunteer ran up to her. "Telgram for you at the central office."

"Telegram?"

"You know, message," said the volunteer who looked at her oddly. Leah had volunteered to work at the hospital in the refugee camp to help make the days shorter. Otherwise there wasn't too much to do except wait.

She hurried to the office, and a bored-looking secretary handed her an envelope. Leah found the message worded strangely:

LEAH STOP IAN AND I ARE ASSIGNED BACK TO CAMBODIA STOP
WE'RE GOING TO MAKE A SIDE TRIP TO KAO I DANG TO SEE YOU
IN FEW DAYS STOP ROZ STOP

Except for the part about stopping, she could figure out the message, and she felt a surge of excitement about seeing her friends again. There were people at the camp who had become acquaintances, but a refugee camp was not a place to create permanent relationships. It was a place where people came and went, and waited in between those times.

While she was sitting, thinking about this, a nurse beckoned to her, giving an order. At least here one was busy and useful, and there wasn't too much time to think.

She was in her quarters, shared with several other women in a barracks-like building, when someone shouted, "Visitors! They say they're looking for Leah De Bernay. Anyone named that here?"

"That's me," she said. "They can come in." She ran forward to hug Roz and then Ian. They looked the same. Maybe a little leaner, a little more travel-worn.

"I'm sort of surprised you're still here," said Roz. "I thought maybe you'd have gone out to find a place for yourself. You're bright enough. You could do it."

"I was going to," said Leah, "except that someone brought me word of the children. I was told that five children had been brought to the *sahakor*, a cooperative, near Siem Reap in the Northern Sector at about the time Scorpio was . . . about the time I returned to Phnom Penh. It could be them. The area is right."

"Or it could be any five children," said Ian. "Didn't your source give you any names?"

"No, everything I hear is rumor, and I'm worried because I've been hearing some very troubling things from those escaping the new regime."

"We've heard the rumors, too," said Roz, "of forced work, starvation, even in some cases torture and murder."

"I can't bear to think of them in that place alone," said Leah, "with no one who cares for them. And I'm trapped here with no way to get to them."

"You do have to take into account," said Ian, "that in a case like this, people exaggerate some of the things that might happen on an occasional basis, turning what is only a bad situation into a horror."

"If even a tenth of the things I've heard are true, it is a horror," said Leah. "When I hear these things, I want to cross the border and go to Siem Reap myself, to see them."

"Maybe you want to go, but think about it before you do anything so foolish. I doubt if you'd make it past the border."

"I don't really have any idea of playing at being a hero or rescuing them. I just want to see how they are. If I saw that they were living happily among their own people, then I could go away without even trying to contact them."

"I see," said Roz thoughtfully. "It just might be possible."

"What?" asked Leah, rising from her chair. "How would it be possible?"

"What you're thinking might not be a good idea, Rosalind, my girl," said Ian. "Especially if we were caught in the deception."

"I told you we had been re-assigned to Cambodia, but that wasn't accurate. Everyone has heard the rumors coming out of there. It makes the country sound like a hellhole. Pol Pot, who has finally made himself known as the leader of the Khmer Rouge, has felt the pressure of world opinion. He's invited us—well, not us personally, of course, but a corps of reporters from various countries—to tour the country and bring our stories about Democratic Kampuchea, as he calls it, back to the world. He wants to scotch those rumors, once and for all."

"But you said there was a chance that I could get back there."

"Another harebrained scheme," said Ian. "I can't listen to this." He put his hands over his ears, but he was grinning.

"You go with us, as part of our delegation," said Roz. "We'll need a passport for you, but fake papers are easily come by in this neck of the woods, for a price. Ian's right that this is fairly harebrained, and it could also be dangerous."

"I don't care about that."

"As you said," Ian added, "this isn't supposed to be a chance for someone to make a dramatic rescue. Just an opportunity to set your fears at rest."

"Or to find out the worst," said Leah. "But either way, I want to know."

With a sense of unreality, Leah looked from the plane's window as it landed at Pochentong airport. In the camp she had often dreamed of going back, and everyone talked about it. "When I go back," they would begin, as if it were a foregone conclusion that soon they would return and pick up their lives where they had left off. She had been able to accept the plane ride, which was only her second, as if she were a seasoned air traveler. After all, if you didn't look out the window and see fields of clouds spread out below, you could convince yourself that there was nothing magical about the ride.

The clothing Roz had bought for her was stiff and unfamiliar: gray slacks and a red jacket. Wearing trousers always made her feel like she was masquerading as a man. In the shoulder-slung pouch Roz had bought, she carried the false papers. She had the idea that as soon as she came off the plane, people would start pointing at her and shouting that she was an imposter.

But, of course, when it came time to deplane, no one was paying the least attention to her. There were journalists and delegates from half a dozen countries invited as the guests of Pol Pot. They were met on the runway by a small crowd. A native orchestra struck up a Cambodian folk tune, and several healthy-looking children were out front, carrying small red flags and bouquets of flowers, which they presented to some of the more important delegates.

After the ceremony, the party was broken up into smaller groups. Leah's group, which was made up of herself, Roz, Ian and two Chinese reporters, was conducted to the edge of the runway where two sleek, black cars sat waiting for them.

"Mercedes, no less," said Roz. "It looks like they're going all out, but I'm anxious to see what the city looks like."

They drove down Monivong Avenue, Phnom Penh's major thoroughfare. Leah was amazed to see that everything looked clean and beautiful. In the city she had left, signs of war had been everywhere. Barbed wire had surrounded government buildings, streets and parks. Now she saw no jeeps, antiaircraft guns or bunkers—things which had been in plain evidence before. She saw a few guard stations as they drove along. Painted as they were in bright colors, greens and golds, they didn't look as if they were serious military buildings.

In fact, it looked as if all artifacts of war had been swept from the city. Along the main street, buildings had been freshly painted in pastel colors with pots of flowering bougainvillea and frangipani set out before them. A park they passed was immaculate—lawns mowed, flower beds tended and blooming colorfully.

There was no litter on the street, but that wasn't surprising since there wasn't much traffic, either. She remembered landing here and being in the midst of teeming traffic. *Where are the bicycles, the buses, the people?* she wondered.

She began to have an eerie feeling as the car moved along the broad avenue, as if the buildings they passed were merely facades. If you really looked at them closely or went around in back of them, you'd see they were only cardboard, propped up in back by poles. *No, the plane ride got to me, I guess,* she thought. *I can't fault a government for keeping the city neat.*

Soon they arrived at the guest house that had been assigned to them. It was located on Monivong Avenue and had evidently once been a private residence, though it was large. Roz wandered around the suite she and Leah were to occupy, opening drawers and poking into cupboards.

"It seems they were ready for the incursion of Western journalists," she said, "or at least the female contingent." Her search had turned up three bottles of nail polish, four tubes of lipstick, and a big bottle of cheap perfume. "But they didn't provide any soap. I guess we know what they think of our personal habits."

"We have to give them a chance," said Leah. "I don't believe they would have invited this many foreign reporters if they really had anything to hide."

"You may be right, but when I thought of what Phnom Penh had been like before, the ride out here began to give me the creeps. I know things weren't perfect here. There was plenty of poverty, crime and the like, but there used to be a certain excitement walking down these streets. The people used to be laughing and yelling, buying stuff from street vendors. Now the place looks like a ghost town."

Leah felt uneasy about the way Roz's impression echoed her own, but she was determined not to prejudge the situation. She was just here to look and listen.

On their way down to the evening meal, Roz joked with Ian about the cosmetics she'd found in her suite.

"That's nothing," he said. "My suite is next to a liquor cabinet—well stocked, I checked. And the drawers are all full of Cambodian cigarettes."

"Guess they knew your preferences," said Roz.

The dinner was a formal sort of affair, even though the group was small. Uniformed servants attended the table, bringing in several different courses. The fare wasn't bread and rice gruel, as one might expect in a country that elevated peasants to the most important rank, but a style of cooking at once native and yet elegant. They also met their guide, Sieu Thirith. He was very much at home in this formal setting. Taller and lighter skinned than most of the Khmers Leah had met, he showed a definite Western influence in his dress and manner. He wore a small clock on his wrist, though that was a practice Leah had noted before in this age.

What made it more obvious in Sieu's case was that he had a habit of consulting it, even in situations when the correct time wasn't needed. Back would go the cuff and his eyes would seek the clock's face as if the wisdom of the ages were to be found there.

Conversation during the meal was somewhat restrained. Sieu did most of the talking, informing the guests about the abundant rice harvest and providing statistics on the burst of productivity that had occurred once the new regime had taken power.

Toward the end, one of the Chinese journalists dared to ask a question about human rights.

"There is no problem about human rights," said Sieu, surreptitiously consulting his watch. It tended to give listeners the impression that Sieu's mind was on some future duty more important than the current conversation. "A few disgruntled members of the old Lon Nol government complain, and the reporters are suddenly clamoring about human rights. I ask you, what about the peasants and workers who are now so much better off under the new regime? But you will see."

The next day Roz and Ian wanted to visit some of their old haunts. Leah accompanied them for awhile, but soon went her own way, wanting to see places she was familiar with. As she left Monivong Avenue and journeyed down side streets, she realized that her impression of the avenue as a stage setting was strangely correct. Here on the side streets, where well-kept shops and residences had been left empty, the yards were weed-choked or filled with mounds of debris. When she reached the old Central Market where she and Scorpio had gotten their first impressions of this world, she saw that it had been planted with banana trees. The vending stalls sat empty with the green fronds of trees jutting out of them.

As she stood looking at this, she heard the squeal of tires and saw that one of the Mercedes sedans had stopped behind her. Sieu motioned for her to get in, so she did.

"I should have cautioned you and your friends that it's not a good idea to travel about on your own. This is why we have bodyguards accompanying our party." He looked at his watch.

"I'm sorry," said Leah. "I didn't know there'd be any danger. In fact, everything seems amazingly quiet here."

"Our relations with our neighbors the Vietnamese aren't good just now, and there is always the danger of terrorist acts. I'm sure you can imagine the trouble that could be caused by the wounding or the death of even just one foreign journalist."

Leah told him she understood perfectly, yet in all her wanderings she had seen nothing threatening. She wondered if the threat could be what she might see while traveling around on her own. She was sorry she wouldn't get to return to the children's old hideout, but it had probably been cleared away by now in the spirit of good housekeeping that seemed to prevail in the city.

When she returned, she saw that Roz and Ian, too, had been summarily rounded up and returned, and their tempers were the worse for it. There was little time for them to vent their anger, however, Sieu announced that a trip had been arranged to the Institute for Scientific Training and Information.

As they arrived, they were greeted by a young man who went by his revolutionary name of Kaun. Sieu had told them that Kaun was only twenty-eight and was the president of the college. This rapid promotion of the young to positions of responsibility was something Leah would see over and over, as, she supposed, a reflection of Pol Pot's "great leap forward."

Kaun welcomed them and took them on a tour of the school. In a classroom hung with banners reading "Diligence and Determination!" and "Forward, by Leaps and Bounds!" and other inspirational slogans, Leah saw several children at work threading wires into a mechanical device. While they looked well fed and otherwise well cared for, their faces were solemn as they concentrated on the difficult work.

"Educating engineers the old way is wasteful," said Kaun. "These children learn intricate mechanical tasks by rote, and can then be put immediately to work."

"But when do they play?" asked Leah.

Kaun looked at her as if she were speaking a foreign language. "Playing is reactionary. It doesn't help us to create a high standard of living," said Kaun haughtily. "We are all asked to sacrifice, and we do it gladly to build the new state."

Leah was pretty sure nobody had asked these children if they wanted to sacrifice for the state, but she didn't say so.

"Some scientific institute," said Ian on their trip home. "Our friend Kaun was spouting nothing but nonsense about engineering. And I don't know about you, but I'm getting a very bad feeling about this whole trip."

Roz and Leah began talking at once, spilling out their fears and suspicions.

"Neither of you would be familiar with an American television program called "Mission Impossible," said Roz, "but the Mission Impossible crew was sometimes hired to set up illusory scenarios. Detail by detail, they would build up a false image for their victim, and at the end, they would let the illusion unravel, much to the victim's chagrin. I have the feeling that any moment I'll turn a corner and see one of Pol Pot's men hard at work creating another stirring picture of revolutionary Kampuchea for us to see."

"But what can we do about it?" asked Ian. "We're not allowed to go anywhere that isn't approved by Sieu, or talk to anyone without him acting as translator or go-between."

"We do what we came here for," said Roz. "We look and listen. Maybe something will unravel and then we can go home and write what we've learned."

"We're scheduled to visit some cooperatives when we tour the countryside," said Leah. "I hope one of them is the one I was told about, near Siem Reap."

The journey by car was leisurely, following the Mekong River, with various stops along the way to tour factories and plantations. There were picnics in the green countryside. It might have been like a vacation trip, except that there was always that sense of unreality, the foreboding feeling that around the next bend there might be a sight they were not supposed to see.

Occasionally, they would catch a glimpse of emaciated people with swollen bellies, but the car never stopped. The fleeting sight of something disturbing slid by, to be almost but not quite forgotten. They were shown groups of well-fed workers in fields and factories, looking industrious, under banners bearing the ever-present slogans.

The closer they came to Siem Reap, the more excited

Leah became. But she was stunned when one morning Sieu made an announcement.

"I'm afraid our scheduled visit to the cooperative today must be cancelled," he said.

"You can't," said Leah. "We were promised."

"It's quite impossible." His eyes sought the solace of his watch. "Everyone is in the fields, tending to the harvest." She suddenly realized that checking his watch was a nervous gesture meant to mask a lie, and that he was lying now. "Besides," he added. "We have already visited a cooperative."

That part of what he said was true. Leah remembered the model village they had been shown. A cluster of well-built Khmer huts on stilts, furnished with fresh straw mats and a few solid pieces of furniture. The cadre assured them that families lived together: mothers, fathers and children. Families were not separated, despite the rumors. There was a large communal dining hall in which the reporters were allowed to eat. It was plain fare, but there was plenty.

"We will visit instead a foundry for smelting agricultural implements," said Sieu. "Now I'll bid you all good night, so that you can be rested for our journey tomorrow."

"Yes, plenty of rest," said Roz. It was only late afternoon. They were often dismissed like this to fill time as best they could. Roz and Ian got out a well-worn deck of cards. Leah paced as they slapped the cards down on the table between them.

Am I to have come so near only to go back without seeing them? Leah asked herself. She knew it was only a few miles to the cooperative. An easy drive.

She yawned and stretched. "I guess I am pretty tired," she said. "Maybe I'll take a nap until dinner."

"I hope you're not too disappointed about not going to the cooperative," said Roz as Leah turned toward the bedroom.

"I'm disappointed," said Leah, "but there were no guarantees. I appreciate all that you two have done for me."

"What is this, a testimonial dinner?" asked Ian. "Let's play cards."

Once in the bedroom, Leah put some clothing under the blanket so that if anyone looked in it would seem as if she were still there. Then she climbed out the window, hiding behind some flowering foliage as she worked her way over to one of the cars. During the trip, she had become interested in the motorcars. The chauffeur had been puzzled when she had asked him where the crank was, since she had last ridden in a crank-started Russian car, then he had exploded in laughter when he realized she thought the Mercedes needed to be cranked to start. Then he had demonstrated with pride how the machine worked, and Leah had paid careful attention. She had only been interested before, but now operating one of these cars was crucial.

She looked about for the guards as she crossed an open space to the car, and had to crouch down behind the vehicle when a servant crossed the lawn.

There was no key in the ignition of the first car, so she went on to the second, but walked more softly as she realized that one of the chauffeurs was catching a nap underneath the car. He was evidently forbidden the use of its interior.

When she looked inside, she saw that he had failed to take the keys with him when he had sneaked under the car for a nap.

Quietly, she entered the car and eased the door shut. For a moment she sat there in confusion, having forgotten everything the chauffeur had said about starting the car. Then she remembered.

The car spun out of the drive, jerking and squealing in response to her inept efforts to control it. Looking into the rearview mirror (*a miraculous invention,* she thought), she saw the man who had been sleeping under the vehicle sit up and wave his arms about wildly. Immediate pursuit didn't worry her too much. The servants would have to go to the masters before it was all sorted out, and it would take them some time to figure out who had the car and where she was going. Once she had accomplished her purpose, she supposed they would catch up with her, but there wasn't too much they could do to a visiting journalist except deport her. Once she had seen the children and knew they were all right, then it wouldn't matter.

Chapter
12

*F*or awhile Leah veered about on the road, threatening other vehicles, but it was late in the day and the road wasn't well traveled. Twice she stopped to get directions from people she saw along the roadside. They looked at her as if she were an apparition.

The dinner hour came and went, and she supposed that by now everyone knew what she had done. She hoped Roz and Ian weren't too angry, though this might mean that everyone in the tour would have to leave. They had probably learned all that Pol Pot would allow, anyway.

Finally, she came to a gate that led into the grounds of the cooperative. The place looked as if it were fenced all around in barbed wire. There was a padlock on the gate but no guard. Leah solved this problem by backing up the big car and running it toward the gate. The weathered wood cracked and went down under the tires. She rolled on over it and approached a group of Cambodian-style huts, except that these were old, the wood warped, and the thatched roofs moldy and half fallen in. A few people came out of the huts as she drove in and looked at her dully. They looked half starved and wore rags.

Leah began to run from house to house shouting, "Chi, Siv, Khieu—children, where are you? It's me, Leah!"

She could hardly believe it when she saw Chi appear in a doorway, and behind him Siv. Then they were all spilling from the hut and surrounding her, calling, *"Ma! Ma!"*

After a moment Chi looked around and said, "I think the cadre are busy overseeing the second shift of the evening meal, but we'd better go inside to talk."

Leah was surprised at how much all the children had grown. They all talked at once, trying to bring her up to date. In the excitment of their meeting, Leah had not taken note of her surroundings. The inside of the hut was worse than the outside. The straw mats were moldy, and when she moved one, a mouse streaked across the floor. The stains of leaking water were traced across the walls and floor. The children didn't look as emaciated as the people Leah had seen earlier, but they were all thin, giving their eyes a hollow look that hurt her. Their clothing looked like the bits and pieces of a wardrobe cast off by adults. The sight of their thin arms and legs sticking out of oversized shirts, shorts and dresses could have been comical, but in this situation it wasn't.

"You all look pretty well," said Leah, "under the circumstances. Is the food here good?"

The looked at her numbly, as if her question didn't make any sense.

"When we first came," said Siv, "things weren't this bad, and we had enough to eat. Then they told us the rice harvest had failed, so all we would have was rice gruel."

"It was more water than rice," added Khieu.

"Anyway," said Siv, "things would have been awful, except that Chi, and sometimes others of us, would sneak past the barrier at night and forage for food in the jungle."

"Adults are stupid, aren't they?" said Phal. "Even we know that it's almost impossible to starve in the jungle."

"We had to be careful, though," said Chi. "We would have been punished if we had been caught."

"We were lucky, too," said Khieu. "They usually separate the families, but they didn't know we were a family, so they just let us stay here together."

"We kept thinking of you and Scorpio, and how you would have wanted us to try and stay together. I kept telling the others that someone would come and rescue us, and now you're here."

Now I'm here, thought Leah. *And I didn't have any plans beyond getting here and seeing the children.*

"You're going to take us away with you, aren't you?" asked Siv, and all the rest crowded around her.

"All right, yes, we're all going to try and get out of here." As they climbed down out of the hut, Leah's lack of planning became painfully obvious as she saw several men with rifles walking around the car and peering into the windows.

"Maybe you'd better go back into the hut while I talk to these men," said Leah.

Three rifle barrels pointed in Leah's direction as she approached the car. "I'm with the delegation of journalists," she said, handing one of the men her passport. "Unless you want me to write a very unflattering story about you, I suggest you point those the other way."

The man held her passport upside down and looked at it, ignoring her threat; he looked as if he didn't know a journalist from a fence post. "You must take this up with *Angkar Leu*," he said, and his companions laughed.

She knew this meant, roughly, "higher authority," but she didn't like the sound of their laughter. When they gestured toward a cinder block building in the center of the compound, she had no choice but to go there.

When she came through the door, she saw a small, wizened man with round glasses sitting behind a desk. He acted as puzzled as the others as to her identity and purpose, and her threat of writing a negative story received the same chilly response. When he looked up at her, the lamplight made his glasses opaque. It was like staring into two golden coins.

"I have been told nothing of this," said the bureaucrat, "but it will all be investigated in due time. For now I'd like to study your papers." Leah was about to remove the papers from her purse, but the man put his hand out, meaning that she should give him the whole purse.

Reluctantly, she handed it over.

"She will occupy one of the rooms in the back until all this is checked out thoroughly."

"Room" was a euphemism for the cubicle she was taken to. It was a sort of cell with a cot, a table and chair as the only furniture.

At least I've seen them, she told herself. *That part was not a disaster. I've seen them and they're all right. Soon Sieu will come and explain everything and they'll let me out of here.* Though the bed wasn't inviting, she had grown tired, so she lay down and was soon asleep.

She didn't know how much later it was when she heard the cell door open and saw Sieu appear, along with the man in glasses.

"Sieu, I'm glad to see you," said Leah. "Please explain to these people who I am. I want to get back to the tour."

"I'd be interested in knowing who you really are," said Sieu, "but there will be time to find that out."

Leah was shocked to find him almost a different person now. He did not give his watch a fleeting glance. Instead, he stared at her with an arrogant honesty, as if he was glad to leave lies and masks behind for the moment.

"I want to get back to the tour at once," said Leah, hoping

she didn't sound as desperate as she felt. "If you detain me here, my friends are going to have to ask a lot of questions. It won't look good when the stories come out." She wondered why she kept trying that threat, since it hadn't worked so far.

"Your friends have already been here," said Sieu. "They were very sad to hear that in your ill-conceived plan to steal a car and run away from the tour, you had an unfortunate automobile accident. They were adamant about seeing the body, of course, being the curious sort of people they are, but as I explained, it was not possible for official reasons. There was little they could do. They had to be satisfied with taking away your personal effects and the promise that your body would be shipped home for burial. Of course a great many mix-ups can occur in such an arrangement. The tour itself has had to be cut short, but I believe we have done a good job of, as the Americans say, public relations."

"But what can be gained by keeping me here?" said Leah.

"For one thing we can find out why you left the tour so precipitously," said Sieu.

Leah almost told them that she'd come here to see the children, then thought better of it. She didn't want them involved in this.

"It may be just a reporter's natural curiosity," said Sieu, "which I need not point out can get one in a great deal of trouble, if that curiosity is not curbed. Or there may have been a hidden reason. It's no secret that the American C-I-A."—he emphasized each letter—"has infiltrated Cambodia. I suppose you know nothing of this."

"I don't have any idea what it is," said Leah.

"Now, no one is that ignorant," said Sieu. "But, as I said, there will be time to establish your identity and your motives."

The man in glasses (Leah still had never heard anyone call him by name) walked over to the table and put down pen and ink and a sheaf of papers. "We often have prisoners write their life history. It forces them to focus on their transgressions."

He gestured toward Leah, indicating that she should sit down at the table, and so grudgingly, she did. He looked at her expectantly until she picked up the pen and began to write. Under the twin moons of his stare, she couldn't think of a plausible lie, so she began: "I am Leah de Bernay, daughter of Doctor Nathan de Bernay, a Jewish physician in Avignon in the fourteenth century."

The man in glasses was too far away to read these words, so he nodded approvingly. "A good beginning. We will leave you to your work." While she continued to write, they went out.

Now that Leah knew she wasn't getting out of this room, she felt claustrophobic. It was also painfully obvious to her that she had now seen too much to be released. This was the very story they had worked so hard to keep a secret. *All I can do now is keep the children out of it,* she thought, as the pen continued to scratch over the paper. As she began to tell of her travels with the alien, Scorpio, she began to concentrate on him as she hadn't done since she'd seen the mine go off. In some way, she began to feel, Scorpio was close to her again.

Chan mounted the horse and was surprised when it burst into a furious gallop. He grabbed its neck and hung on as it ran down the road at a breakneck pace. Once out of sight of the palace, he hauled back on the reins and dismounted. He hadn't wanted to admit to Mey that he'd never ridden a horse before, but galloping off on his mission had seemed the gallant thing to do. He looked at the horse trailing behind him on the rein, and thought about unsaddling it and letting it find its way home. Then he thought better of it. He'd need something to barter for a trip across the Great Lake.

Even though he was afoot, he made good time and was soon searching for Scorpio near the peasants' hut where he had left him. It took almost a full day, but he finally located Scorpio at his camp overlooking the lake. As Chan approached, he saw the alien sitting on the shore in a full lotus, either deep in meditation or looking out across the water.

Considering the importance of his errand, Chan didn't stand back and wait for Scorpio to finish his meditation, but went and grabbed him by the shoulder. The startled alien must have acted on reflex, because Chan found himself grabbed and tossed to go rolling down the bank.

"That was . . . very good," said Chan as he rose and dusted off his clothing. "I was afraid you'd forgotten all I had taught you."

"I have forgotten nothing," said Scorpio, "especially how you stole my orb and abandoned me."

"I felt sorry about that later, but I thought you'd soon come seeking me out," said Chan.

"I was otherwise engaged," said Scorpio. "Besides, I've found what I wanted here—peace, serenity, and an end to conflict."

"I'm glad to hear it," said Chan. He pressed the orb into Scorpio's hand. "But you have to come with me. There's about to be a war. I've promised Queen Mey that you can use your orb to make her side victorious."

"You shouldn't make rash promises. The orb isn't a weapon," said Scorpio. "I'm afraid there's nothing I can do."

"I told her you'd think of something. Otherwise she will have to marry some dolt and she'll be lost to me forever. I've come a thousand years to find her, and I'm not going to give her up now. If you're really set on your life of solitary contemplation, then you may have it. Good luck to you." Chan turned and started away.

"Wait," Scorpio said. "I think I've contemplated enough. All I could think about was Leah and the children, anyway. I'll go with you. Maybe we can think of something. But I warn you, I don't travel alone anymore."

Scorpio looked out over the water, and Chan followed his gaze. To Chan's amazement he saw the familiar glider-like shape of a pteranodon, twenty-foot wings spread wide as it made for the shore.

"Where did that come from?" he asked, and then remembered that day on the island and the golden eggs he had found. "Can't we use the orb to take it back?"

"Too late," said Scorpio. "It's now used to the climate and wind currents of this world. It's found a new home and a parent." Chan was surprised when the pteranodon came to shore and hopped toward Scorpio, giant wings jutting awkwardly upward.

"Whenever I tried to leave camp, Wings and I have had a bad effect on the natives," said Scorpio.

"We can't help that," said Chan. "We have to start back now or we'll be too late to avert the war."

Queen Mey watched Pan pull up the war chariot before the palace. This was the day she had been dreading. Pretending a bravado she didn't feel, she climbed into the chariot amid the gathered troops and gave the signal to advance. Pan had been right, she observed. A good quarter of the troops had defected at the thought of going into battle behind her, although loyalty to the royal family kept the rest of them there.

Pan didn't look around at her as he drove the horses. There was no question that he would be at her side in what would probably turn out to be a dangerous confrontation, but she could tell that he was mightily disappointed in her decision to go through with the battle.

She had put this moment off as long as possible, hoping that Chan would return with the sorcerer he spoke of, but there was no sign of him. When word came that Satha's army was approaching the city, there was no choice but to go out and face him. Anything could have happened to Chan, she realized, though the nagging feeling wouldn't go away that he had simply abandoned her.

Perhaps she deserved it, but she had dreamed such dreams. Not since she had danced in the temple courtyard in hopes of dreaming of her lover had she been so giddily romantic.

The chariot rattled over a hill, and now she could see the ragged line of Satha's army—much larger than she could have imagined. She patted Pan's shoulder. "Won't be long now, will it?" she said, and he did look around then, as if he understood her meaning. In the forefront as they were, neither of them was going to withstand this first charge.

As they drew nearer, a rain of arrows fell around the chariot. Mey sent her own shaft winging in answer. Then for some reason the enemy stopped firing.

She looked back and saw a chariot breaking through the ranks of her own army. Two figures were in it, and the driver either drove like a madman or the horses were fear-crazed, for they ran flat out over a rocky patch of ground, bouncing the chariot madly and making the riders cling to its sides. At this pace, the madman's chariot was overtaking her own.

Satha's army was stopped in its tracks, but they weren't looking at the demon chariot, but upward, into the sky. When she looked up, she caught her breath. A creature such as she had never seen was gliding there, keeping pace with the madman's chariot. Its strange appearance must have been what was giving the mad warrior's horses their speed, because as the winged thing came near, all the horses around her began to lay back their ears and fight the traces.

She heard Pan mutter under his breath. "The air dragon!"

The demon chariot had now easily caught up with that of the queen, and as it dashed past, she saw that Chan was the driver, and with him was another creature with the face of a *naga*. It was surely the sorcerer he had spoken of, but Mey had expected him to be at least human. She also saw that Chan exerted no control whatsoever over the crazed horses, and though he was trying to stop them, they continued their runaway pace, right toward the forefront of Satha's army. The dragon continued to sail serenely over them, as if he followed Chan.

"And I thought him a common street rogue," said Mey. "What a warrior he is!"

"He has the blood of the dragon," said Pan, pulling up on his own horses to watch the effect of the air dragon on the enemy troops.

Satha's army began to break apart as the dragon flew toward them. In moments it was a complete rout, even though Mey's army had simply stopped to watch the spectacle. When her men saw that the enemy army was retreating, they remembered their duty and began to chase the fleeing troops, adding injury to insult whenever possible.

After awhile Mey saw Chan and his friend returning from the battlefront, minus their chariot but with the dragon above them as if it were a kite drawn on an invisible string.

"You were just in time," said Mey, leaping from the chariot to put her arms impulsively around Chan. "And your air dragon is wonderful."

"We arrived too late at the palace, but I talked your ministers into giving me a chariot so we could catch up," grinned Chan. "If we do this again, I hope somebody will give me lessons on how to drive horses."

"You won't need to drive horses in Democratic Kampuchea," said Scorpio.

"Democratic Kampuchea? Where is that?" asked Chan ironically.

Pan put all of them into the queen's chariot and returned them in triumph to the Great City, the dragon keeping pace with them overhead.

Chapter
13

*A*fter the processions were over and the feasting scarcely begun, Scorpio saw Wings safely housed in a high tower where he could come and go as he wished. Because he was reluctant to return to the festivities, Scorpio paused in the courtyard of the as-yet-unfinished temple complex, to try and resolve something that had been bothering him.

He had told Chan that when he was lost in introspection during his brief foray into contemplative life, he found himself thinking of Leah. Sometimes it was the children, but it was mostly Leah, and he had felt that she was close to him despite the distance through the years. The contact felt strong, despite the fact that he was without his orb. Now that he had it back, he wanted to try again.

As he paused near the temple, where Siv had once seen a figure dancing by moonlight and a very proper young Communist leader had dreamed a dream, Scorpio began to feel that he was making contact with Leah.

He felt that she was very sad. Yes, there was that, but there was more. She was in a very bad place, and she was in danger. *Leah, please tell me where you are,* he thought, *and I'll try and come to you.*

As he stood there, orb in hand, trying to make contact, he had just begun to receive the message when there was a flash of light brighter than that of the moon, and a familiar figure appeared, framed in a translucent aura.

Lethor the Hunter left his orb-craft and stepped forward. "You don't know how hard it was to find you. I was in and out of every era in this bedamned world, but now that you are using your orb again, I was able to find you. You won't escape again."

Scorpio stood calmly, watching the Hunter come nearer.

"You may remember, Aquay, that when we met earlier, I told you that I was offering you the supreme tribute a Hunter can give: the honor of being killed with these hands."

"I do remember it," said Scorpio, bowing to his adversary, though of course the Hunter had no idea of what such a gesture might mean, "and I'm waiting."

Scorpio's self-possession inflamed the Hunter, and he made a growling noise and charged, reaching for Scorpio's throat. "It'll be a pleasure to wring that skinny neck!"

To Scorpio, it was almost as if his body acted on its own. As the Hunter's huge hands closed on his throat, he thrust both arms up stiffly, breaking the Hunter's hold. Following up, Scorpio moved in closer and drove his knee into the Hunter's abdomen.

Lethor doubled over in pain. Scorpio felt as surprised as the Hunter looked. *It works!* he thought. *I really defended myself.* But his triumph was momentary, for the Hunter recovered quickly and was coming at him again. And this time he was really angry. Scorpio realized that the element of surprise was gone. If he didn't bring the Hunter down quickly, the being's superior strength would begin to tell. As the Hunter swung a fist toward his head, Scorpio countered with a high block, and then grasping a handful of the Hunter's cloak, pulled the being toward him as he delivered a powerful kick.

Struck solidly on the head, the Hunter staggered backward, hit the temple wall, and slid to the ground. Scorpio took the ready stance, waiting to see what would happen. The Hunter only lay there groggily, even his aggressive temperament dampened.

He lay there as Scorpio lifted his own orb. All during the fight, Leah's message had been coming through. Now he knew where she was and something of the danger she faced. He could delay no longer.

As the orb-craft encircled him, he felt a terror worse than that of facing the raging Hunter. The abyss began to open beneath his feet. He had half-decided to deactivate the orb when suddenly an image formed before his eyes: a small pteranodon making itself look foolish by honking plaintively from the edge of a precipice while its folded wings jutted skyward. *Am I forgetting my wings?* Scorpio asked himself. *I pity myself for being alone in an alien world, but when have I been alone, really? Leah and Chan and so many others have accepted me, even though I look strange to them. They support me, buoy me up when I would otherwise fall.*

Scorpio took one look into the abyss at his feet, and then stepped off into Igre's endless gullet.

Leah sat in her cell and waited. She had turned over the lengthy document she had written to the man with glasses, and she supposed he was reading it. It had done one thing for her: she felt better about losing Scorpio. She hadn't been able to face the idea that after all their travels together he was gone, and she had to go on from here alone.

When she wrote about his death, she felt that she had finally accepted it, although the sense of his presence had also increased, and for some reason she had pinpointed her own location, beginning with the cell itself and working outward, as if she were creating a psychic map.

The door groaned inward and the man with glasses returned. Sieu was with him, and both of them looked flustered and angry. While Leah watched, Sieu grabbed the pages she had so laboriously written and tore them once, twice, and flung them at her feet.

"What is this drivel? Travels through time, an alien creature, a magical orb," said Sieu. "Do you take us for complete fools?"

That didn't seem to be a question to answer just then, so Leah remained silent.

"We will have the truth!" shouted Sieu. The man behind him stood by, and taking off his glasses, cleaned them on his shirt. It was the first clear glimpse she had had of his eyes, undistorted by the lenses, and she didn't like what she saw. The horror stories from the refugee camp begin to come back to her in greater detail.

She thought at first that fear was making her hallucinate. The light in the room, always dim, was becoming brighter. She knew it was real when Sieu and the man in glasses began to look around nervously.

The orb bubble formed itself in the center of the room, with Scorpio at its heart. He had usually looked flustered upon landing because of his incomplete control of the orb, but now he looked uncharacteristically calm as he dropped lightly to the concrete floor.

"Your message told me you were in danger," he said, "and I suppose these two are the problem."

"I didn't send a message," said Leah. "All this time I feared you were dead or lost in some forgotten era."

"This thing isn't human," shouted Sieu. "Quickly, keep it busy and I'll summon the guard."

As Sieu fled, the man in glasses looked around in confusion, then he regained his composure. Swiftly, he stepped between Leah and Scorpio. "You have no right to be here," he said. "I arrest you in the name of the People's Army."

As the bureaucrat approached to take him into custody, Scorpio, feeling quite confident, lashed out with a sudden snap kick. The small man looked startled, but reacted by fending off Scorpio's blow with a low cross-block, then he threw a kick of his own that left Scorpio's arm numb to the shoulder. Scorpio realized that the few lessons he had had probably left him out of his depth with this man, who looked small and skinny but now jumped about like a venomous spider.

For several moments they sparred, each taking the measure of the other. Scorpio felt pressured by the knowledge that reinforcements would be along shortly. At last Scorpio's greater reach began to tell. He battered the man's head with a series of quick hammer-fist punches, and then finished him with a side kick that sent him flying into the concrete wall.

"What are you staring at?" he asked, turning to Leah, though of course he knew. Like everyone else, she had seen him as an eternal victim. *Well, she'll have to get used to the change,* he thought. *For that matter, I'll have to get used to it.*

Scorpio and Leah heard the sounds of voices, the scuffle of feet in the next room, but he was extending the orb to her. The light brightened again, and they jumped.

Leah was surprised to look around and see the towers of the temple complex, not in ruins but new and impressive for all that things didn't look quite complete yet. But her surprise at the temple took second place to what was perched on the topmost tower, preening its white wings. It looked down, and upon seeing them, gave a loud squawk and dived.

"It's coming for us!" shouted Leah. "Take cover."

Scorpio only laughed and stood in the shadow of those giant wings until the creature had made a pinpoint landing beside him. It scrabbled across the ground in a way Leah found horrible, and fawned at Scorpio's feet.

"I'm not complaining, mind you, but I thought you were afraid to use the orb."

"I remembered my wings," said Scorpio cryptically.

"But bringing me away isn't really enough," said Leah, remembering the children. "What about Chi and Siv and the rest? That's an awful place. I can't just leave them there."

"I suppose I can bring them here as well," said Scorpio, "but it will take five trips."

"Then you must begin at once. Wait—where is here? Or should I say when is it?" Then the freshly built temple gave her a clue. "This is still their country, I guess it will be all right."

"I think we have to do it," said Scorpio. "Show me that map again."

"What map? Oh." Leah concentrated on the layout of the cooperative.

Scorpio disappeared in a sphere of light, and several minutes later came back with Chi. The boy came blinking into the light of what must have seemed to him to be a new world, though it was actually an old one. Leah received him with open arms. Soon he was looking curiously around and was making a slow approach to the pteranodon. Soon he sat stroking its soft fur.

By this time Chan and Mey had joined them in the courtyard. By installments, Mey was told the children's story, and she too began to welcome them as they appeared one by one in her domain.

Seeing the children's starved condition and lack of care, Chan said adamantly, "Something has gone terribly wrong in Democratic Kampuchea. It is not for this that we all sacrificed and hoped. If I had ever entertained thoughts of returning, they're gone forever."

Queen Mey clapped her hands and several servants came running. "Take these children to my private apartments and treat them like honored guests. They are to have the best of food, clothing—everything."

"I'm thinking of the other children we left behind," said Leah as Scorpio appeared with Vanna, the smallest, in his arms.

"I'm afraid this is all," said Scorpio with some alarm. "We can't empty the future into the past. We don't even know what problems we might be causing down the timeline with the meddling we've done already."

"I suppose it's all we can do," said Leah, cradling Vanna in her arms and following the royal retinue toward the palace.

Scorpio looked around the temple complex. What he had done did weigh upon his mind, but, he supposed, the centuries that would grind down this mighty edifice would also be forgetful of six young people and a DP, a displaced pteranodon.

Several weeks later Scorpio and Leah rode an elephant in a procession that rivaled the one that had concluded the crowning of Queen Mey. People along the concourse cheered and pointed upward to see the great air dragon soaring above them. They had come to accept the beast as a symbol of their deliverance from Satha's army, and Wings had become a familiar sight on his way from the tower in the temple complex to the Tonle Sap.

Chan and Mey rode the royal white elephant, for this was a twofold occasion: their wedding day and the crowning of Chan as Chandravarmin II. Scorpio looked back to see the children riding an elephant behind his. They looked as if they were having the time of their lives, and they were regally dressed as befitted members of the royal retinue.

"Do you think they're really happy here?" asked Leah.

"What does it look like to you?"

"I guess I'm overprotective," said Leah. "Maybe it's time to give up ideas of being their *Ma*."

"Maybe it is," said Scorpio. He realized that vestiges of his uneasiness had begun to impinge on Leah's mind. "Cambodia is a pleasant land, and I think Chan would like us to stay on as his chief sorcerers or somesuch, but it will never be home to either of us. We both have unfinished business elsewhere."

"Are you sure that jumping won't bother you, even a little bit? Remember Igre's gullet."

"Why should it? I'm not a naughty little fry. I'm an adult Aquay with a mission to accomplish, and if that means fighting, so be it. As long as somebody else is the aggressor, of course," he added, more in the vein of the Scorpio Leah was used to.

"Let's stay on for awhile, at least," said Leah. "Just to be certain that the children and Wings are adjusting well."

"Chi is working on inheriting my role as Keeper of the Dragon, I think," said Scorpio. "And the other children are always playing with it, putting garlands of flowers about its neck and the like. But if you wish it, we can stay a bit longer, I suppose."

The coronation and wedding were both lavish affairs, with many rituals and sumptuous garments and much chanting and swinging of censers. Scorpio had to admit he was getting a bit bored with it, when there was a sudden increase of light in the chamber. Startled wedding guests shrieked and fled, as an angry-looking red figure appeared and began to cast about as if looking for someone in the mob.

"Lethor!" said Leah. "I thought you told me you'd bested him in hand-to-hand combat, and we wouldn't have to worry about him anymore."

"I guess he's more tenacious than I thought," said Scorpio. "He must have been off somewhere regaining his courage. We'd better get going. I think that this time he's going to be using his laser. We'll have to forego the honor of being killed with his hands."

"I think I can do without it," said Leah.

At this point Lethor must have spotted them, because he raised his wrist and a laser beam seared across the room. Leah had never seen him shooting with such abandon, as if he had lost all his Hunter's poise and no longer cared about ethics or etiquette. It didn't matter how many others were hurt as long as he could see Scorpio dead. He continued to send beams hissing in their direction as he chased the terrified crowd before him.

"He's going to hit someone by mistake," said Scorpio, and held out the orb to Leah.

Chan had leaped from the throne to put himself between Queen Mey and the disturbance. The sight of them, frightened but locked in each other's arms, was the image Leah took with her as the orb whisked her away.